PLACE OF MISTS

PLACE OF

A Talos Cord Adventure

MISTS

by Robert MacLeod

The McCall Publishing Company
New York

Library of Congress Catalog Card Number: 78-122146
SBN 8415-0058-4

The McCall Publishing Company
230 Park Avenue, New York, N.Y. 10017

PRINTED IN THE UNITED STATES OF AMERICA

For
Marion and Jim

I

Sneaking in across the East River, the rain squall hit
Manhattan when it was least expected. Blotting out the
skyline, it lashed down on the regular Tuesday afternoon
protest crowd picketing the United Nations frontage on
First Avenue.

Soaked to the skin, placards abandoned, they scattered
in the battering downpour.

The mounted cop who'd been keeping them circulating
stayed where he was. Huddled deep under a waterproof
cape, he made quiet, sympathetic clicking noises to his
horse. It moved restlessly and brought a hoof down on a
fallen placard, punching a neat hole through the already
sodden demand 'Freedom Now for Middle Europe'.

The cop grinned with no particular malice and squinted
round at the low, rain-swept bulk of the General Assembly Building. Water ran from his cap and down the back
of his neck. He swore softly, wondering what the delegates had been chewing over this time. The session should
be almost finished.

Some day, he decided, he'd have to bring the kids along. They could take the guided tour, finish with coffee and doughnuts in the basement cafeteria and a look around the souvenir shops.

Shifting again in the saddle, he frowned. A couple of picket people still remained, sheltering in a doorway across the road. At least, he guessed they were picket people. They were swarthy, one had a small neat beard, and they ignored an empty cab which went cruising by, screen-wipers slapping.

He tapped the horse with his heels, moved a few yards, then stopped again. What the hell, they were only shelter-ing, they looked harmless enough—and hadn't his own grandmother come out of Rumania or some such place?

Shrinking deeper under the cape, cursing the down-pour, he patted the horse's bedraggled mane.

Over in the doorway, the taller of the two men let out a long, slow sigh of relief, glanced at his companion, and nodded.

Three minutes passed. The rain began to slow, the ragged tail of the squall appearing above. As if it was a signal, the first limousine with C.D. plates began rolling out of the U.N. complex, carrying delegates homeward.

Flying the Union Jack, a dove-grey Rolls-Royce was first away and in an obvious hurry. The British delegate had a dinner date up-state. Next came two Cadillacs, filled with small Asiatics chattering like monkeys. The men in the doorway watched them indifferently, then tensed as a long, low Mercedes nosed out. It flew a green and gold flag. A uniformed chauffeur and two passengers were aboard.

Still moving at little more than a crawl, the Mercedes came opposite the doorway—and a hand grenade, five-second-fused, lobbed with practised skill, exploded in

8

vivid fury under the front wheels.

The car heaved, lurched, swerved on burst tyres and stalled. Another grenade hit the road a yard short and exploded as the driver's door flew open. Gun in hand, the chauffeur caught the full blast and was tossed back· behind the wheel like an outsized rag doll.

The tall man was running, a Luger pistol held ready, ignoring the mounted cop's shrilling whistle and the sound of hoofbeats. He reached the Mercedes, wrenched open the rear passenger door, fired twice, then turned.

The mounted cop wrestled his .38 Special clear of its holster and out from under the cape. He triggered first, reined hard, then fired again as the tall man, staggering back, tried to bring the Luger into line. The second bullet spun the stranger round and down. He lay where he fell.

Two prowl cars came heading in, sirens rising to a wail. Blue-uniformed guards were spilling out of the U.N. buildings. The mounted cop remembered the other man, sawed on the reins, hefted the .38 in a new arc. Then he froze.

The other man hadn't moved. Framed in the doorway, he had another grenade in his hands. For a second, maybe more, the bearded face split in a clench-toothed triumph. The hands flickered, pulled the pin and clutched the grenade to his chest.

The new explosion whipped tiny splinters of metal across the roadway. A fragment grazed the horse along one flank. Squealing, it reared and almost threw its rider.

Then the violence had ended, the prowl cars were skidding to a halt, the rain had stopped. One of the U.N. guards reached the grenade thrower's body. He looked and turned away, gagging. Chest and head had gone, the trunk ended in a red mash of flesh.

Heart still pounding, the cop swung down from his

saddle. The man he'd shot had taken both .38 slugs high in the chest and was dead. He had a light, coffee-bronze skin and thin, eagle-beaked nose.

Scowling, the cop peered through the Mercedes' open doors. The chauffeur was dead, uniform blasted to rags. The nearer of the rear-seat passengers was slumped back, a bullet-hole neatly between his eyes, an unfired automatic clutched in his right hand. The third man, small, fat, with a pock-marked face, had fallen forward between seat and floor. Blood was oozing down the front of his tailored suit. As the cop watched he twitched, moaned, and went still.

One corner of the cop's mind noted that the car's occupants had the same light, coffee-bronze complexion. But the rest suddenly filled with the enormity of what had happened.

He damned his Rumanian grandmother, the United Nations, the weather and his luck with impartial fervour. Tucking his pistol away, he swallowed hard, and prepared to begin explaining.

. . . . .

'Minister of State, brother-in-law of their president— and now we've got to ship him home in a box!'

Fat jowls quivering, face flushed an angry red, Andrew Beck smashed his hands flat on the desk. They were short, powerful hands, black hair sprouting along the backs from the wrists down, hands typical of the man who ruled as head of the U.N. Field Reconnaissance section.

Talos Cord made a sympathetic murmuring noise from his post near the window and laid down the evening edition with its glaring headlines. The TV set in the corner had the sound turned down, but the picture tube was once again showing newsfilm of the grenade attack aftermath.

'A dead Arab V.I.P., a political powderkeg, an all-round panic—all because some policeman decides to hold Be Kind To People Week.' Bitterly, Andrew Beck left the worst part till last. 'And the thing happens on our own damned doorstep.'

'The cop nailed one of them,' reminded Cord mildly, watching the older man, trying to gauge what was coming. Fifteen minutes had passed since he'd arrived at the 39 storey slab of blue-green tinted glass and aluminium which was the Secretariat Building. The assassination two hours old, First Avenue was tidy again.

'All right, he did. And the other one blew himself up. Who cares?' grated Beck. 'Both were suicide squad material. They didn't expect to get away. Their job was to kill Atalan Said, finish.'

The middle telephone of the three on the desk began ringing. Beck ignored the summons, though the red bands painted along the receiver signified the direct line from the Secretary-General's office. It shrilled on for some thirty seconds, then stopped.

Talos Cord grimaced slightly, a lop-sided expression which creased across his strong-nosed face to halt at the old hairline scar which ran like a thin crescent across his left cheek. He took one of the fat, yellow-leafed Burmese cheroots from his top pocket, but left it unlit.

Plenty of 'phones were ringing that evening in the Secretariat Building. The assassination of Atalan Wat Said, special Assembly delegate from the Arabian republic of Jemma, had caused turmoil in a dozen different departments.

But Field Reconnaissance was in most trouble. Field

Reconnaissance, the U.N.'s special intelligence unit, the 'peacemaker' section which existed to sift rumours and whispers, hints and jealousies, distil out fact, report the truth—then make its own moves, take its own action wherever trouble threatened.

This time something had gone wrong.

There was a light tap on the door and it opened. Beck's secretary, a honey-skinned, high-breasted Eurasian girl with silky black hair, neatly rounded bottom and long, slim legs, came across the room and laid a file on the desk. Beck's single grunt covered thanks and dismissal. Her face remained serenely expressionless, but as she turned away she gave Cord a wink which came and went like a camera shutter.

It took a lot to throw Aila, decided Cord as she went out. But then it normally took a lot to throw Beck.

The Field Reconnaissance chief flicked through the file. Cord switched his attention to the vast map of the world which occupied all of one wall, a map with a thin scattering of pins—four, maybe five per continent—which marked where Field Reconnaissance's slender strength of operatives were located. Only one pin was currently back at home base, his own.

'Sit down somewhere,' said Beck suddenly, his voice still harsh. 'And either light that thing or put it away.'

Unruffled, knowing the man, Cord found a chair and obeyed. He felt Beck's eyes rake him from the blue-grey Donegal sports coat he wore with a grey roll-neck shirt to the tan whipcord slacks and moccasins. The rest, to the outsider, was a slim, easygoing, muscular figure. Just over medium height, age shading onto thirty, Cord was built on compact lines. Clean-shaven, black hair cut short, he had a wide, humorous-lipped mouth and lazy dark eyes.

The desk-lamp of Beck's desk threw a glow which picked up the scar, made it a line which seemed to highlight rather than mar his features.

Beck sighed, leaned back, and for a moment the fat, untidy man showed his age.

'You know what today's Assembly agenda was about?' he asked, not waiting for an answer. 'Finance—with Atalan Said leading the usual parade, saying we'd have to economise.'

Cord nodded. Not for the first time the U.N. had money troubles, was desperately in need of funds. But for plenty of delegates the basic creed seemed that it was better to receive than give. Their objective was to put the screws on the major powers, force them to make a last-minute rescue operation. The same delegates stuck inflexibly to instructions from home. Disobedience could mean a rapid disappearance from the cosy Manhattan flesh-pots.

'Money.' Beck made the word sound an obscenity. 'That bunch of old women down in Finance have been trying to whittle our appropriation for long enough. They'll rub their hands over this mess.'

Cord decided to light the cheroot. He worked it over carefully with a match, then asked bluntly, 'Why was Said killed?'

'That's going too fast,' said Beck grimly. 'Start with the main picture—and pay attention. This one is going to be all yours.' He heaved out of his chair, plodded over to the map-wall, and stabbed a thick forefinger at the Arabian Peninsula. 'Take away Saudi Arabia and the Yemens, who squabble like hell anyway, and what's left in this parish? A layer-cake of little states, the frontiers drawn with a ruler and machine-gun in the old colonial days. Maybe it worked then. But not now they're independent.'

On the eastern edge of the boot-shaped Arabian Peninsula, the Democratic Republic of Jemma showed as a narrow slice of territory with a useful outlet coast on the Persian Gulf. Cord frowned at the map, searching his mind for what little he knew about the area. It was outside the oil-rich sector, probably just so much rocks, scrub, sand and heat.

'The basics are simple enough,' rumbled Beck, tapping the map again. 'Among Jemma's next-door neighbours the one that matters is Daman, to the south. They've the kind of boundary line where a patrol shoots first and checks passports later.'

'The old-fashioned friendly touch,' murmured Cord. He waited, knowing Beck couldn't be rushed in this mood, that he'd get around to things in his own way.

'Tribalism plus politics,' corrected Beck, turning away from the map. 'Jemma is eighty per cent Banu Khala tribe with a Mahhabi minority. Daman is almost one hundred per cent Mahhabi—and what matters is the two states were one kingdom until the First World War, with the Mahhabi running things and kicking the Banu Khala around.'

'And Daman would like to see things that way again?'

Beck nodded. 'Except that Jemma has its own ambitions when it comes to possible takeover. They already knock hell out of their Mahhabi minority over any excuse that comes along. It happens Atalan Said had charge of the "Mahhabi problem" until the end of last year.'

Cord whistled softly, understanding now. 'And the two characters who killed him . . .'

'Flew into Kennedy International last week from Cairo on Egyptian passports,' said Beck grimly. 'That's about all we know. But I don't think the Egyptians are involved.

14

They've got more than enough on their hands, got their fingers too badly burned in the last Israeli business.' He stopped and shrugged. 'Want me to spell out how the republic of Jemma is going to react to the murder of one of her favourite sons, who they're going to blame?'

Slowly, Cord shook his head. Turmoil and bloodshed, burning villages, hunted fugitives—if that hit the Arab state's Mahhabi minority it would almost certainly bring rapid escalation into a bushfire war with Daman. The kind of war which could spread far and fast, drag in plenty of outsiders as old loyalties, old hates, broke through in the Arab world.

Beck rasped a thumbnail along his stubble-shadowed chin. 'Well, at least the Secretary-General has moved fast enough. Both states are in line for sizable UNESCO aid programmes and need them badly. He's telling them straight that if they want the aid projects they'd better keep the brakes hard on.'

'That might work, for a time anyway,' mused Cord. 'How do they shape if it doesn't?'

'Militarily?' Beck's frown deepened at the prospect. 'Let's say a lot of people are interested in the answer. They're fairly even on manpower. But Jemma's army is U.S. equipped and British trained while Daman went the other way—Russian equipment, Chinese instructors.'

Cord swore with some feeling. 'Then it's going to be a busy little corner. How soon do I leave?'

'For Jemma?' Surprisingly, Beck chuckled. 'You don't. I want you in Morocco. Aila's made the reservations. You've a couple of hours to pack a bag and untangle your sex life.'

'But . . .' Cord blinked, bewildered.

'Morocco,' repeated Beck firmly. 'That's where President Sharif of Jemma happens to be right now. Full name Mohammed Sharif, aged about sixty, normally tough as they come. But he went down with virus pneumonia a month or so back and he's convalescing in the Atlas Mountains—courtesy of the King of Morocco.'

'And you think someone will try for him next?' Cord couldn't keep the doubt from his voice. 'Why? It's on the cards that the Atalan Said thing was strictly a vengeance killing, levelling off some old scores.'

'Maybe, but I'm not taking that chance,' snapped Beck, losing some of his scanty patience. 'Mohammed Sharif runs Jemma, stop. If he sees sense and keeps things cool we may get out of this with nothing more than a few riots. But if another squad of Mahhabi extremists happened to land a grenade on Sharif's lap then Jemma and Daman would be at each other's throats by next morning.'

Cord nodded his reluctant acceptance. 'All right, but he'll have his own guards along. And the Moroccans run a tight security service of their own. So what's left for me to do once I'm out there? Unless . . .' he stopped, mashed the cheroot stub in an ashtray, and regarded the Field Reconnaissance chief with a slowly gathering suspicion. 'There wouldn't be something else, would there?'

'Only incidentally.' Beck cleared his throat with an unusual embarrassment. 'You'd have found it mentioned in the briefing details. Sharif has almost finished his convalescence, but he's due to visit a couple of local U.N. projects before he goes home. There's a UNESCO backed nuclear power plant on the coast and a soil erosion thing inland. The idea is he should get some first-hand knowledge of what a UNESCO aid deal could do for his country. And—ah—obviously we don't want anything to go wrong.'

'I'm sure we don't,' agreed Cord with a wooden-faced

solemnity. 'It could be fairly unfortunate.'

An almost sheepish grin began to form in the corners of Beck's mouth then was firmly incorporated into a more familiar scowl. 'All you've got to do is keep Sharif in one piece until he climbs on that plane to fly home. And if trouble starts to shape don't take anything or anyone at face value.'

The middle telephone began ringing again. Beck grumbled under his breath, and padded across to answer.

.   .   .   .   .

Two hours wasn't a lot of time. Talos Cord collected a thick manilla envelope from Aila in the outer office, smacked her rump in a way which brought a yelp and a giggle, then headed out of the Secretariat Building.

First he had to do some explaining to a certain redhead from Virginia and cancel the promising plans they'd roughed out together. She had an apartment just off Sutton Place, which meant a three-minute-walk followed by half an hour of pleasantly mutual sympathy. From there, he took a cab to the quiet brownstone hotel along Lexington where Field Reconnaissance kept a permanent booking. He packed a bag, tidied the rest of his stuff to leave the place clear for the next man home, left the keys at the downstairs desk, and was on his way.

The helicopter air-coach service from the Pan-Am building to Kennedy was over a New York already meeting the February dusk with a twinkling challenge of lights. Idly, Cord watched the scene slide past below, thinking of Beck down there, wondering what he might have been doing if that fat, untidy figure hadn't slammed uninvited into his life.

The chopping blades slowed. His stomach tightened for

17

a moment as they began to drop down towards the Kennedy runways. No, he didn't like air travel. Never could, never would. But it was the same as a lot of living—inevitable.

Flight PA 541 for Rabat, Morocco, via Lisbon took off on schedule minutes after nine p.m. As the silver-hulled Boeing jet clawed skyward Cord glanced with satisfaction round an almost empty first-class section, switched on the tiny reading lamp above his seat, and got down to the briefing in Aila's envelope.

Most of it was as Beck had outlined, except that he'd be met on arrival—and for once there was no real cover story to hide his purpose. Beck's strategy appeared the primitively effective one of throwing him in, hoping his presence would precipitate its own reaction.

There was a single, cryptic footnote. 'Where possible, vouchers must in future accompany major expense items.'

He was still chuckling over that one when the cabin staff began coming round with drinks. The stewardess who served him wafted Chanel and promised dinner wouldn't be far behind. Cord tucked the papers away, looked out his window once, saw the ghost-like outline of a gently quivering wing, and drew the curtain quickly. That way, he could at least try to pretend he wasn't six miles up.

With the time-change jump, it was 8.40 a.m. when the Boeing made a brief touch down at Lisbon. Another hour in the air and they'd crossed the North African coastline. Below, Morocco appeared at first as a splotch of dark green streaked with a winding rust-like ribbon. In the distance, the high peaks of the Atlas Mountains were tipped white with snow.

They came lower. The landscape shaped into a surprisingly fertile stretch of fields and woods, the red streak becoming a winding, muddy river. Wheels down, the Boeing banked over a city with plenty of tall, modern buildings glinting in the bright sunlight.

Rabat International Airport wasn't much to look at by any standards. Once landed, the jet taxied in towards a cluster of low, anonymous buildings. There were the usual vividly painted refuelling trucks, a couple of fire engines and the inevitable scatter of parked aircraft . . . most of them piston-engined jobs belonging to Air Afrique or Royal Air Maroc. As they stopped, outside life seemed mainly composed of blue-uniformed airport police with holstered pistols.

From the 'plane, he followed the others across a warm, dusty stretch of concrete and into a small, shabby waiting room which had a picture of the King of Morocco on one wall. The outside door was closed firmly once they'd entered, and a long time passed before an inner door opened and passengers began funnelling through immigration.

When his turn came, Cord placed his passport before a young, bespectacled Arab immigration clerk whose neat European suit had the tip of a red silk handkerchief showing discreetly from the breast pocket.

'*M'sieu* Cord'—he gave a quick murmur of interest and looked up from the passport—'good. Someone is waiting to see you.' He beckoned, and a burly figure in police uniform crossed over. The clerk carefully stamped Cord's passport, returned it, and nodded to the other man. 'For Major Rucos.'

Shepherded along a short corridor, Cord passed what looked like the main customs area. Then his escort stopped, knocked ponderously on a door, opened it, and gestured him through. The man stayed outside, closing the door again once he'd entered.

The room was small, unfurnished except for a table, and had sunlight pouring into it through a high, metal-framed window. Puzzled, Cord took another step forward then heard a throat gently cleared almost behind him. He spun round.

The man was dark-haired, small and thin, in army khaki with major's insignia. The usual holstered pistol was absent. Instead, he had a short, ivory-handled swagger stick attached to his left wrist by a loop of braided leather thong. The face was fine-boned, a neatly clipped black moustache on the upper lip, the eyes a startling bright blue, sharp and penetrating. The rest was that crisp, formidable manner small men can so often make their own.

'My apologies for the surroundings, Mr Cord.' The voice was quiet, level-toned, and devoid of accent. 'My name is Rucos—Major Rucos. I thought privacy might be preferable to comfort—normally our Customs Department use this room to search the occasional suspect traveller.'

'As long as I'm not in the suspect category,' nodded Cord easily.

'You, Mr Cord?' The Moroccan gave a faint, polite shrug. 'At the moment I wish I knew. If I explain my present task is the security of a certain visiting Head of State, you may understand what I mean.'

'I'd hope it puts us on the same team,' said Cord cautiously. 'You know why I'm here?'

'Of course.' Major Rucos produced a pack of cigarettes and offered them. As Cord took one he fed another between his lips, accepted a light, and drew hard on the smoke. 'A diplomat is assassinated in New York one day and a United Nations man arrives here the next. The conclusions are obvious.'

'Just conclusions?'

Slowly, Rucos shook his head. Stick still dangling, he tucked the cigarette pack away and carefully buttoned down the pocket flap. 'You are from something termed Field Reconnaissance section. According to instructions received by your UNESCO project director you have absolute charge of security arrangements during President Sharif's visits to these projects.' The blue eyes narrowed a little, the almost pedantic voice went on. 'I will presume that should be interpreted as absolute charge of U.N. originated arrangements only, as approved by the Moroccan government.'

Cord nodded, diagnosing a mild case of upset pride. 'That's pretty much the way I see it, major,' he said soothingly. 'We've no cause to quarrel.'

'Good.' Major Rucos inclined his head but gave no particular sign of thawing. 'Then you should enjoy your stay. Most strangers find this a fascinating country, rich in interest. And friendly—provided they do not embark on ill-advised ventures.'

'A warning, major?'

'Perhaps,' agreed Rucos. 'For if you were to act foolishly, if you were to—well, disappear, you would become my responsibility. I have enough responsibilities without more.'

'I'd hate to have you overworked,' murmured Cord with a heavy irony. He strolled over to the window. Outside, a line of small, thick-stemmed palm trees separated them from a road busy with traffic. 'All right, major. You're efficient. You've got yourself a man somewhere inside the UNESCO project and probably a whole lot more in other places. I'm ready to believe you've got President Sharif wrapped up like he was in a cocoon. You're doing your job. Why not let me do mine?'

'For whose benefit, Mr Cord?' The army man's mouth tightened. 'For whose credit? Your own people's—to make up for damaged prestige?'

'If that's the worry, you can have any glory going,' said Cord wearily.

Major Rucos jerked. The swagger stick suddenly slammed his anger against the table. Cord ignored him, flicking ash from his cigarette, watching it fall towards the bare wooden boards at his feet.

'Cord, for that suggestion I could have you marched aboard the next aircraft leaving Morocco. *Ya salaam* I— we are no longer anyone's colony, we are not people to be treated like children . . .' Rucos's voice slowed and died away, puzzled.

Talos Cord had stopped listening, was standing staring at a spot just below the windowsill. Beckoning in silence, he dropped to his knees. Frowning, uncertain, Rucos came over.

'Maybe you're right, major,' said Cord in a loud voice. 'I'll stick to the project security problems, and the rest is yours.'

As he spoke, he put a finger to his lips and then pointed. Taped under the protruding windowledge, the 'bug' microphone was about two inches long, not much thicker than a pencil, and with a short wire tail like a wasp's sting. He saw Rucos's face wrinkle in startled understanding and turned again towards the microphone.

'You don't seem to believe me, major. But I'll prove it if you wait until tomorrow morning.' His hands were moving rapidly, delicately, freeing the 'bug' from its tape, gently bringing it clear. 'We got a little out of one of the New York assassination team before he died—maybe just enough if a hunch I have is right. I'm hoping for names, major. They'll be yours to do what you like.'

He'd found the screw-thread. His fingers twisted and the midget transmitter broke into two sections. Relaxing back on his heels, he looked up at Rucos.

'End of message, major.' He made a sad, reproachful noise. 'And I thought you wanted privacy!'

The Moroccan glared out of the window, as if hoping to see something which might help, then gave a tight-lipped grunt.

'Over what range would that operate?' he demanded.

'Four, maybe five hundred yards.' Cord hefted the pieces in his hand. 'Efficient little jobs. They use a mercury cell battery lasting eight or nine hours. The receiver can be in a car, an office, someone's pocket, anywhere.' He grinned ironically. 'Looks like the opposition is more organised than I imagined.'

'Arabs are no longer so many primitives on camels,' said Rucos with a bitter depth of feeling. He sighed. '*Aywa* . . . yes, Mr Cord, I owe you at least a part apology.'

Cord shrugged. A fat black fly had appeared from somewhere and was making a lazy business of crawling across the opposite wall. Still watching it, he asked, 'How many people would know you'd use this room?'

'Several—mostly airport staff. I arranged it by telephone this morning.' Rucos paused for a moment then went on very quietly. 'I will find our more about this, I promise.'

'Whoever planted the microphone is likely to try and get it back,' said Cord thoughtfully. 'Why not leave it where we found it, simply make things look as if it developed a fault? That can happen.'

Rucos nursed his swagger cane for a moment then nodded. 'And we will know who comes. I will arrange that.'

'Good.' Cord glanced at his watch. 'Someone called Jackson should be waiting for me outside. Unless—are you still planning to toss me on a 'plane?'

'No, and it was not intended,' confessed Rucos. 'Your presence has been approved at too high a level. Jackson is the project deputy director—he has been told you are having slight trouble over Customs clearance.' He fell silent, gnawing his thin moustache, then asked, 'What you said after you discovered the microphone—there is no chance it was true?'

'None.'

'I see.' A strange expression on his face, the soldier looked again at the tiny transmitter. 'But now someone is going to be very interested in you. I can have men nearby —live bait is a good way to hunt, but only a fool would leave a tethered goat unguarded.'

'Old Arab proverb?'

'*Imazighen*, Mr Cord,' corrected Rucos. 'Berber, like myself. There is a difference.' He produced a folded green beret and placed it on his head. 'I'll come with you to the Customs line. After that, I can always be contacted through any gendarmerie post.'

'And we're co-operating?' queried Cord.

'For the moment, and on this matter only.'

'Temporary truce.' Cord grinned, his fingers busy again on the transmitter bug. 'Fair enough. Better stay quiet. This thing is working again from—now.'

He taped the little unit back in its hiding place then

they tip-toed out, easing the door shut behind them.

The small, tight-lipped figure led the way from there, Cord following and outwardly cheerful.

But he sensed it wouldn't pay to have any illusions about Rucos. Pride was only part of the major's package. Underneath lay a dispassionate ruthlessness and something else, something Cord didn't quite understand.

He'd have to find out more about Major Rucos. Even a goat had the right to know which direction the hunter's gun might be pointing.

2

Walter Jackson, deputy director UNESCO special projects group, Morocco, was a surprise. Six feet tall, bald, built like a bull, he walked with a stick and a heavy limp and looked around fifty. When he spoke, it was with a nasal Australian drawl. When he laughed, which seemed often, the sound boomed and his red face appeared in danger of splitting. His frayed slacks and crumpled fawn jacket looked as if they'd been slept in a few times.

'Customs clearance, they said.' Jackson gave a loud, derisive chuckle. 'Like hell—I saw Major Rucos's jeep and driver outside. How'd you make out, Cord?'

'You couldn't call it an official welcome.' Cord picked up his bag again as Jackson rammed on a floppy linen hat. The UNESCO man limping in the lead, they set off towards the air terminal's exit. 'We agreed to differ on a couple of things.'

Jackson bellowed his appreciation. 'Rucos isn't so bad. We've had him around a few times lately. But he's worried stiff at the chance of something happening to President Sharif. Maybe we all are—though for my money Sharif is a louse.'

'Why?'

'You'll find out,' said Jackson cryptically. They left the building, passed a bus unloading a group of Moroccans, and he gestured towards the car park opposite. 'Transport's waiting. And while I remember, Joe Palombo—he's project director—sends his apologies. He's in town, but there's a conference scheduled with some Government brass. Now, you want to see Mohammed Sharif straight off, right?'

'Sooner the better,' agreed Cord.

'That's what I figured.' Jackson cleared his throat and spat expertly into a withered-looking floral border. 'Well, he's at Mihmaaz, a place in the mountains about a hundred and forty miles from here, on the edge of the ski resort country. We can do it in a shade over three and a half hours, which is respectable. Try for less, and you're liable to start hitting things.'

'Three hours will do.' Cord grinned, liking the man, wondering about that limp, noticing the beads of perspiration already on his forehead though the temperature was only pleasantly warm.

Grunting approval, Jackson guided him over towards a big, late-model Ford station wagon. Coloured red, it had the usual blue-and-white United Nations badges on front doors and tailgate. A young Arab emerged from behind the wheel, rolled the cigarette in his mouth to the furthest corner, and jerked open one of the back doors.

'Meet Roder Hassabou, the worst damned driver in North Africa, since the time of the old Eighth Army,' declared Jackson cheerfully. He pointed a warning finger.

'Roder, our visitor's a sensitive man, like me. Remember it—no Grand Prix stuff this time. Right?'

'Will do, Mr Jackson.' Unperturbed, the younger man extended his hand. '*Ahlan-w-sahlan*, Mr Cord. Welcome to Morocco.'

The words came slowly and carefully, the grip was light but friendly. Roder was around twenty-five, decided Cord. Maybe a little older if you judged by the eyes. Wiry, medium height, with a thin, high-cheeked face and a lightly pock-marked skin, he was in shirt and slacks. A multi-coloured woollen cap sat far back on his head.

Jackson had moved round to the front passenger seat. He heaved himself aboard in a way which suddenly made sense of the limp, pulling the right leg in after him with a two-handed flick—the mark of a man well used to an artificial limb.

'Let's move,' he said, settling back. 'We've someone else to pick up. Ready, Cord?'

'Ready.' Cord threw his bag into the rear of the station wagon and climbed in. He glanced back at the Arab, caught a surprisingly thoughtful stare which switched immediately into a casual, easy-going grin, then the door was slammed shut. Roder slouched his way back behind the wheel and a moment later the Ford was moving.

'First time here?' queried Jackson, levering himself round.

Cord nodded, wincing a little as the Ford slammed up through the gears. It took the feeder junction onto the main highway in a way which brought a horn-blast protest from a truck driver, and took the route signposted for Rabat city .

Jackson grinned. 'You'll get used to it. How's your Arabic?'

'Just about zero.'

'Well, French will get you by with any official, and a few of the town Arabs speak some English. Right, Roder?'

Roder tyre-screamed round a bend then nodded solemnly. 'Too right, Mr Jackson. Just like you say.'

Cord caught his eyes in the driving mirror. The expression was dead-pan.

'Next thing is money,' went on Jackson determinedly. 'Money is dirhans, around five to the U.S. dollar. The country—well, conditions are modern in the cities and you can trust most of the plumbing. But go off the tourist circuit and you'll find plenty which is straight out of the Middle Ages, though with transistors and instant coffee grafted on. It can be pretty primitive. Right, Roder?'

Roder frowned. 'People are trying, Mr Cord,' he said awkwardly. 'There are plans, and . . .'

'Plans?' Jackson snorted, suddenly earnest. 'Hell, you trip over plans all over the place. But there are places an hour from here where the average four-by-two peasant reckons he's got it made if he owns a flaming donkey.'

'That's why you're here,' mused Cord. 'As I understand it they've got the natural resources but need help to exploit them.'

'Help, yes. From us?' Jackson shrugged his massive shoulders in a way that threatened his jacket seams. 'Any idea what the financial geniuses back at the Secretariat did to our last appropriation request?'

'Probably the same as they did to everybody else,' said Cord. The car jolted hard on a pothole and he grabbed the seat for support. 'We've all got troubles.'

Jackson gave a slow grimace of mutual sympathy, shook his head sadly, and fell silent.

The outskirts of Morocco's capital was an odd fringe

28

mixture of airy colonial-style villas and miserable mud-brick huts. Then, suddenly, they were travelling slowly through heavy traffic through a bustling, European-style city of tall apartments and office blocks, past hotels and a multiplicity of shops and department stores. The old seemed vanquished—except when a side-street gave an occasional glimpse of the solid, apparently unending rampart of crumbling red wall which marked the start of the old quarter, Medina.

The Ford swung left, travelling slowly along another broad avenue with palm trees as a central strip and parking meters lining either verge. Roder scanned the crowded pavements hopefully then suddenly grunted, swung in to stop at the kerb, and gave two quick, light taps on the horn.

'Here she comes.' Jackson shook his head in comical bewilderment. 'Laden like a pack-mule. Better open that door, Cord.'

He did, and looked around. The passing crowds seemed an equal mixture of pretty girls in short skirts and veiled women in ground-length robes. The men among them were mostly in business suits and lugging a briefcase, with only the occasional *djebba* coat in sight.

'Look out!' warned Jackson.

Next moment a flurry of arms, legs and packages tumbled aboard, almost landing in Cord's lap.

'I made it!' The girl slumped breathlessly on the seat beside him, fair hair tousled, packages scattering. Tall, tanned, almost gangling and lean-hipped, she sat back still panting. Small, firm breasts strained with each breath against the tightly belted dark blue shirt-blouse she wore with oatmeal slacks and low-heeled moccasins. 'Somebody give me a cigarette before I collapse.'

The voice had a Scottish lilt, the hand which took the cigarette Cord offered wore a wedding ring. The fingers were long, the nails cut short but painted a careful blood-red.

'Thanks. You'll be Talos Cord, I suppose?' She smiled as he nodded. 'Then hello. I'm Maggie Delday. I don't usually knock people over.'

'I'm glad,' he said dryly, giving her a light. 'Been shopping?'

'This stuff?' She drew happily on the cigarette, her free hand waving vaguely towards the parcels. 'Yes—for everyone but me. I promised people I'd get things.'

'Next time we'll need a truck,' grumbled Jackson. 'You look more like you've been in a race.'

She nodded ruefully. 'That's near enough to it. I forgot the time. I was having a row over in the Medina—a little man tried to charge me tourist prices.'

'*Ya salaam*—the man has my sympathy.' From up front, Roder let out a quiet sound which could have been a chuckle or a sigh. 'We go now, Mr Jackson?'

'Uh-huh.' As the Ford edged back into the traffic Jackson leaned over the back of his seat. 'Treat her kindly, Cord. Maggie runs the office side of things back at base. Get her initials on a piece of paper and you can order most things. But if she says no, you're wasting your breath arguing. She watches every dirhan.'

'It's in my blood,' she agreed, unabashed. 'Hold on, Roder—take the left turn and show Mr Cord our street.' Switching her attention back to Cord, she explained, 'The Avenue des Nations Unies, they call it. Makes a change to find someone likes us, I feel.'

It was another broad thoroughfare, part of it running beside a high wall which had carbine-armed soldiers posted at the few entrances.

'Imperial Palace.' Jackson thumbed at the domed buildings visible on the other side. 'That's where Joe Palombo is now. He drove up with us this morning, grumbling every mile.'

'Who wouldn't, with a six a.m. start?' queried the girl. 'Don't worry, Mr Cord. We're not blaming you—it happens all the time.'

'How does he get back when he finishes?' queried Cord, watching her burrowing into a deep, bucket-shaped handbag.

'If he finishes,' she corrected. 'We've hit a snag on the erosion project. But if he sorts it out by tonight he can catch a plane over to Marrakech—we're based there.'

'The project group is split in three sections,' explained Jackson over his shoulder. 'The nuclear station is going up north of Safi, on the coast, and the erosion project is near Tazenakht—that's on the other side of the mountains. We use Marrakech as administration base because it lies more or less halfway between them, cuts down on travel.'

'That's the theory, but it doesn't always work.' Maggie Delday brushed a wisp of hair back from her forehead, then held out a small, paper-wrapped package. 'This is yours, Mr Cord.'

'Mine?' He raised an eyebrow.

'Yours—at least, your name is on it.' She handed it over. 'I got it from the counter clerk at the Head Post Office—I looked in as usual, because there's always personal stuff lying for someone in the Poste Restante section.'

His name was printed clearly in ink on one side of the package, which was unstamped. Frowning, Cord stripped away the outer wrapping and opened the small pasteboard

31

box inside. Then he gave a soft, surprised whistle.

'What is it?' queried Jackson with blunt curiosity.

The station wagon's horn blasted. Roder sawed at the wheel and shaved past a cluster of firewood laden donkeys. The old woman with them shouted an insult.

'Cord?' Jackson craned further round. 'Something wrong?'

'You tell me.' Cord showed him the box. Inside, a cockerel's severed head nested in a wad of grimy, bloodstained cottonwool. The blood had dried. He turned towards the girl. 'Maggie, any idea when this was handed in?'

'Ugh.' She wrinkled her nose in disgust. 'Well, the clerk said it arrived this morning—an Arab brought it in and asked if it could go in the U.N. staff box. That's all I know.'

He closed the lid and glanced at Jackson.

'First I've seen,' rumbled the older man. 'But I know about them. Roder, what's the name of that character we heard about—the one who'd like Sharif's head on a plate?'

'*El Aggahr*'—the Arab kept his eyes on the road—'it means The Hunter. He is what I think is called a freedom fighter.'

'He is what you don't call a freedom fighter. Not when you're anywhere near Sharif,' corrected Jackson with an attempt at humour. 'But that's it, Cord. The cockerel's head is El Aggahr's trademark—or warning, if you like. According to Sharif he's number one villain back home in Jemma.'

'Except he isn't there now,' said Cord with a grim emphasis.

Jackson nodded. 'That's the way Sharif has it figured. And whoever he is, this Aggahr must have some pretty good contacts.'

The city was receding. Cord sat silent, swaying with the car's motion, Maggie Delday's faint perfume reaching his nostrils. First a listening bug at the airport, then this. Whoever El Aggahr might be, someone knew a surprising amount about what was happening—and wanted to leave no doubts about the fact.

'The Hunter—well, it's a good name for him,' he said at last. 'He's one item Major Rucos didn't mention.'

'Rucos?' Maggie Delday sniffed and wound down a window. 'He'd be a lot smarter if he didn't have such a chip on his shoulder about Europeans. Our little major wouldn't tell you the time unless it suited him.'

Jackson's laugh boomed, then he nodded agreement. 'Maggie's got it right. But Rucos is a Berber—they're mountain people, proud as hell, the kind who say that compared with them the Arabs only arrived yesterday. Seems he started soldiering with a French colonial regiment, stayed long enough to learn the trade, then took to the mountains and ran a fairly effective guerilla band against them.' The laugh softened to a wry chuckle. 'Morocco has plenty of French back on the payroll again —but people like Rucos find old habits die hard.'

'How many feel his way?'

'A few—maybe more than a few,' admitted Jackson.

'Roder'—Cord found and met the young Arab's eyes in the driving mirror—'what would you say?'

'Me, Mr Cord?' White teeth flashed briefly as the thin, darkly handsome face gave an untroubled grin. 'Me, I just say this U.N. firm pays pretty good.'

·   ·   ·   ·   ·

Whatever else, the French left Morocco with the beginnings of a network of fast, provincial-style roads between main centres. From the coastal plain inland they run ribbon-straight in the best Route Nationale tradition.

Kilometre stones began to whip past as the big station wagon ate distance along the main P.7 towards Marrakech. At first the blur of countryside was a fertile scatter of lemon and lime groves, the roadside edged with fruit-laden orange trees. But the scene changed as they headed south towards the waiting, firming line of white-tipped mountains.

Trees vanished. Villages were fewer, more miserable, sometimes a mere handful of straw and brushwood shelters. The land became a flat, arid arena of broken rock and dusty soil speckled with yellow-green outcrops of cactus and prickly pear. The people changed too—more lean, more ragged, sometimes at work on a stony patch of dried-up earth, using a primitive plough yoked to camels or a cow, more often just watching by the roadside.

It grew hot in the Ford. Maggie Delday produced a pair of sun-glasses and perched them on her snub nose. Jackson dozed off, his head rolling against his chest with each sway of the car. Equally sleepy-eyed, Cord sat silent. Only Roder seemed unaffected, hands nursing the wheel, a constant cigarette smouldering in his mouth.

Two hours passed before they swung off the P.7 and began jolting along a narrow secondary road. The car began to climb. Ahead, the road wound higher and higher until the first hills changed to mountain slopes. They passed sheep grazing on scanty pasture, the temperature began to fall, and an occasional patch of snow appeared near the roadside.

Roder dropped through the gears to tackle yet another corkscrew climb then nudged Jackson. The Australian groaned, yawned, looked around, and nodded.

'Nearly there,' said Maggie Delday. She pulled a mirror from her bag, sighed at what she saw, and ran a comb through her hair. 'Did you tell him what to expect, Walt?'

Jackson turned and shook his head. 'Didn't see much sense in it.' His mouth tightened. 'Just don't be surprised at anything that happens at Mihmaaz, Cord—and if you're like me, keep a grip on your temper.'

The car climbed another ridge, reached a fork, and took the lesser way. Next moment Roder eased back on the accelerator. A barrier pole blocked the track, a jeep with a tall radio aerial beside it, a couple of tents pitched nearby. The two Moroccan Royal Armed Forces men in front of the barrier had their rifles slung in unconcerned fashion—with good reason. A few yards away a heavy machine-gun scowled from a carefully dug weapons pit, its traverse covering the approach, gunner and loader squatting behind it.

The Ford stopped a few yards short. Jackson wound down his window as an officer emerged from the nearest tent. The soldier, a lieutenant, looked at the car, smiled, and came over.

'M'sieu Jackson . . .'

Jackson greeted him with a burst of fluent French. The man nodded, glanced cursorily into the station wagon, then stood back and signalled his men.

'*Tariiq* . . .'

The barrier pole swung up and they rolled through. As Roder accelerated, Cord caught a glimpse of another soldier at the jeep's radio, busy talking into the microphone. There were other outposts among those rocks, other men to be advised of their arrival.

'Stage one,' said Jackson briefly. 'The next bunch are Sharif's men.'

'His mercenaries,' corrected Maggie Delday flatly. 'They're probably the only kind he can trust.'

'Europeans?' queried Cord. They were threading through a narrow pass, the rock heavily veined with milky-white quartz.

'Mostly,' agreed Jackson. 'Personal bodyguard style— he brought about a dozen with him from Jemma.'

The pass widened, becoming a brief valley with the mountains closing in again beyond. To one side, almost sheer rock had a solid blanket of snow on its upper reaches. Opposite, on a more gentle slope, a large house was built chalet-style with cream stone walls and a red tile roof. Other, lesser buildings were scattered to its rear.

Suddenly, a figure in a dark blue battledress and matching beret stepped onto the road ahead. One hand signalled them to stop, the other cradled a sub-machine-gun. The man, a European, slouched towards them not bothering to hide his lack of interest.

'U.N.?' The shoulder patch on the battle blouse was green and gold.

'We're expected,' growled Jackson perfunctorily.

The guard shrugged, walked slowly round the vehicle, stared through the glass at Maggie Delday for a moment, then thumbed them on.

They reached the house, crunched along a short stretch of gravelled driveway, then parked beside a flight of stone steps leading to a broad verandah. As Roder switched off, two men came down towards them. Both wore the same dark blue uniforms.

Jackson struggled out of the car as they arrived, brushing aside Cord's attempt to help.

'Back again, captain.' He nodded a grudgingly friendly greeting to the smaller of the strangers. 'You know Mrs

Delday. This is Talos Cord, the man I sent the message about. Cord, this is Captain Sunner.'

'The—ah—assistance from New York?' Captain Sunner was middle-aged, pale, with a fleshy face, pepper-and-salt hair cut short, and bad teeth. He had a single strip of medal ribbons on his battle blouse and a revolver was holstered by his side. 'Arthur Sunner, ex-Indian Army. I'm military aide to President Sharif.' The mouth twisted in a half-smile. 'Call it number one bodyguard for the moment. I'll be glad to talk to you.'

'We'll get around to it,' agreed Cord. 'First thing I've got to do is say hello to the president.'

'Of course . . .' Sunner broke off as the man by his side, tall and skeleton thin, wearing sergeant's stripes, grunted and nodded past them. Roder had left the Ford and was coming over.

'*Ya walad! Qif!*' Sunner barked the command. As Roder shrugged and came to an obedient halt the fleshy face smiled again. 'We're tightening things up a little, Cord. Your driver stays here—Sergeant Denke will keep an eye on him.'

'Worried about him?' queried Cord.

'Just not trusting any stray Arab, whoever he works for,' corrected Sunner. 'All right, Jackson?'

Jackson sighed, and nodded.

'Well, let's go in.' Sunner gestured towards the steps. 'How was the journey up, Mrs Delday?'

'The usual,' she said neutrally. 'You wouldn't like to search us first, captain?'

Jackson chuckled. Sunner flushed then forced a laugh. 'Your—ah—outfit hides very little, Mrs Delday. I wouldn't think it necessary.'

The score, decided Cord, was roughly even.

It was cool and comfortable inside the house. Leading the way down a long corridor, Sunner explained, 'Some wealthy French *colon* had it built in the old days as a summer house. Afterwards, the Moroccan government fitted it out as a guest-house for V.I.P.s—which couldn't have been better as it turned out. A couple of weeks in this mountain air and anyone would feel a new man. Interested in botany, Cord?'

Cord shook his head.

'Pity. We've some magnificent Alpine plants growing around.' Sunner reached an ornately carved door and nodded to the uniformed man on guard outside. He stopped and glanced at Cord. 'One thing for your benefit. The president is modern minded. But when you sit, don't point the soles of your feet at him. Back in Jemma that rates as an insult.'

He knocked on the door, opened it, and they went through into a large, bright room. An almost full-length window faced out across the valley and an arrangement of couches and cushions occupied most of the centre space. There was a large, open fireplace opposite the window and a heavy desk was angled against the wall nearby.

Cord ignored the rest. What mattered was the man who sat waiting—and the girl standing by his side.

Whatever the truth, neither ill-health nor age had made any apparent impact on the small, round figure who was Mohammed Sharif, President of the Democratic Republic of Jemma, potential fuse in a powder-keg of trouble. He lounged back in a short-sleeved white shirt and loose linen pantaloons, a neat black beard carefully trimmed to emphasise his jaw-line. The face was slightly wrinkled, with a thick-lipped mouth which dropped almost petulantly at the corners. But the small, deep-set eyes were coldly alert.

'Mr Jackson, you honour us.' Speaking in an almost languid drawl, Sharif beckoned them forward.

Cord followed the others slowly, his eyes on the girl, fascinated by what he saw.

Her supple, sun-bronzed body might have been carved from teak in its firm perfection. The face, heart-shaped, held a lazy, compelling beauty hard to categorise. Long auburn hair caught back by a plain tortoiseshell clasp, she met his gaze with an almost insolent smile. Skin-tight black silk trousers were topped by a light green kaftan gown, hip-length, loose and sleeveless.

'Your Excellency, may I'—Jackson cleared his throat— 'may I present Mr Cord, who has been sent by the U.N. Secretariat to offer any help . . .'

Sharif nodded briefly. '*Ahlan wi sahlan* . . . you are welcome, Mr Cord. And you make sure of that welcome by bringing the very charming Mrs Delday.' He glanced at the woman by his side. 'Mathilde, refreshments for our guests. Something long, cool, and non-Muslim.'

She nodded and went off, her walk a sedate rhythm.

'Sit down, please—you too, captain.' The bearded figure waved a small, careless hand around. Two heavy gold rings glinted briefly in the sunlight. As they settled, the thick lips tightened for a moment. 'First, Mr Cord, you perhaps have more news of what befell my unfortunate brother-in-law?'

'Only what was known when I left New York,' began Cord. 'And, of course, our regrets and . . .'

The small hand silenced him with an impatient gesture. 'Apologies are rather late. And I have them already.' For a moment the small eyes bored into his own. 'What happened I regard as blundering inefficiency. Atalan Wat Said is dead. I have a nation crying for vengeance, knowing why he was butchered in this way, knowing who were responsible. What have you to say to that, Mr Cord?'

'Nothing at all, Your Excellency.' Cord met the Arab's startled glare with a stony-faced calm. 'Other people deliver the speeches. I'm not any kind of diplomat. You've a personal security problem and my job is to help, nothing more.'

'I see.' For a moment Sharif's fingers drummed on the cushion by his side. 'Well, Mr Cord . . . what do you think of my arrangements here?'

'Pretty good. With the Moroccan posts on the outside and your own men as an inner skin, everything seems buttoned up. Except'—Cord jerked his head—'except perhaps that window. The view looking out is pretty good. From up that mountain, looking in with a telescopic sight, it could be equally interesting.'

'Excellent, Mr Cord.' Sharif grinned a sober appreciation. 'Tell him, Captain Sunner.'

'Bullet-proof glass,' said Sunner briefly. 'The Moroccans made one or two alterations to the original layout.'

'Quite bullet-proof.' Sharif took a deep breath, his eyes glinting. 'Let us show him, Sunner. On the count of three. One—two—three . . .'

Sharif's hand dropped to his side and came up again clutching an automatic. He fired, the report drowned a second later by the heavier boom as Sunner, on his feet, teeth clenched, triggered the heavy .38 Webley whipped from the holster at his hip. Both bullets hit the glass, starring their impact, then ricocheted wildly.

'Mine this time, Captain Sunner!' Grinning, Sharif shook his head in delight. 'You grow slow.'

The doors burst open. The outside guard came in fast, at a half-crouch, carbine at the ready. He halted sheep-

40

ishly at the scene and shuffled out again.

'Satisfied, Mr Cord?' A half-smile twisting his fleshy face, Sunner reholstered the Webley then gave a fractional bow towards Sharif. 'Your Excellency improves.'

Jackson swore softly under his breath. Beside him, Maggie Delday sat very upright, pale-faced. For the first time Cord noticed there were other tiny star-shaped marks on the window, all of them on the inside.

'Bullet-proof,' he agreed stonily.

Still chuckling like a schoolboy, Sharif blew the last trace of smoke from the automatic's muzzle then tucked the gun away in a gap between the cushions.

'Any more advice, Mr Cord?'

Cord shrugged. 'At the moment, nothing you probably haven't heard before. Captain Sunner will know the most dangerous time is when anyone is on the move. Your car . . .'

'A Rolls-Royce, special coachwork, also bullet-proof. It was a gift from my people.' Sharif broke off as the door opened again. 'Ah—at last!'

Unperturbed, the auburn-haired girl made an almost bored return followed by a houseboy in a white jacket who carried a laden tray.

'Mathilde.' Sharif crooked a finger.

Expression unchanged, still without a word, she took her place beside him.

The drinks were long, iced and gin-based. Cord shifted the grip on his glass, saw the clear impressions of his fingers on the smooth, chilled surface, and waited politely like the rest.

Sharif waved the tray aside and the houseboy bowed, beginning to back away. Next moment his foot caught a loose edge of rug. He stumbled, the tray swayed, and a few drops of liquor slopped from one of the remaining drinks to spatter across Maggie Delday's legs.

'*Muharrig* . . . you fool of a clown.' Sharif took two steps from the couch, cuffed the quivering houseboy across the face, then turned apologetically to Maggie Delday. 'I must humbly apologise.'

'It was nothing.' Biting her lip, she glanced at the servant, now edging towards the door. 'It was an accident.'

'Of course.' As quickly as it had come, the rage in Sharif's eyes died, the lined face smoothed again. He returned to the couch. 'Now, Mr Cord, since you are to have a share in the responsibility of my safety, you should have some knowledge of my programme. Mathilde, tell him.'

Again her eyes met Cord's, this time with something like a challenge. When she spoke the voice was huskily cold and impersonal.

'His Excellency will be in Morocco only four days more —we return to Jemma by air from Rabat on Sunday evening. He has decided to visit the nuclear power station tomorrow afternoon.'

Jackson swallowed. 'Tomorrow? We didn't expect . . .'

'This crisis following my brother-in-law's murder,' shrugged Sharif. 'My health is secondary to my country's welfare. And other matters have arisen. Go on, Mathilde.'

She nodded. 'During the rest of tomorrow His Excellency has matters of state to finalise. Friday will be devoted to prayer and meeting certain business executives who have arrived from Europe. The visit to the soil erosion plant at Tazenakht will be on Saturday, at a time we will advise.'

'Excellent.' Sharif reached out a hand and pinched her on the cheek. She showed no reaction, though when he let go two white patches showed where the fingers had squeezed. 'There are times when I would be lost without this Mathilde. But there is no fear of that, eh?'

'It is unlikely, Your Excellency,' she said calmly.

He nodded approval, then suddenly pointed towards Jackson. 'One thing I want understood. At this electricity place, I have no interest in generators or such things. Only the water plant, this fresh water extraction from the sea. You will arrange it?'

'If that's what you want.' Jackson frowned. 'We would have liked a little longer to make arrangements. Even the security side . . .'

'You've an expert to help there,' reminded Sunner sardonically from the almost forgotten background. 'You're not worried, are you, Cord?'

'We'll manage.' Cord got to his feet, reached into his pocket, and crossed towards the couch. 'Still, maybe the president will be interested in this.' Deliberately, he dropped the little cardboard box in Sharif's lap. 'Take a look. It was waiting for me at Rabat.'

Sharif frowned, looked at him querulously for a moment, then impatiently lifted the lid. Next moment he took a long, whistling breath. The box trembled in his hands—with rage, not fear.

'El Aggahr . . .'

Sunner sprang to his side, saw the severed cockerel's head, and swore harshly.

'Cord if this is some kind of moronic joke . . .'

'A joke?' Sharif was momentarily hopeful, then shook his head. 'No, Mr Cord comes here with apologies, not jokes.' He pushed the box aside, letting it lie between himself and the girl. Her eyes flickered down and for a second she almost seemed to smile.

'You know what this means?' demanded Sunner.

43

'That some of His Excellency's less enthusiastic voters are here in Morocco,' said Cord dryly.

'Renegades.' Sharif's voice rose almost a full octave. 'Renegades or some of those other Mahhabi filth from Daman—by Allah, some day they will all pay in blood. Some day . . .' he stopped, swallowed, and rocked backwards and forwards on the couch, mouth still twitching.

'Captain'—it was Mathilde who broke the silence— 'perhaps Mr Cord should see the other.'

'If His Excellency . . .' Sunner saw Sharif nod, gave a sigh, and turned away. He opened a drawer in a small table to one side and returned with an almost identical cardboard box. 'Cord...'

Cord took it. Inside was another cockerel's head. He closed the lid and handed it back.

'When, captain?'

'This morning.' The blue-uniformed figure forced the words out with reluctance. 'In this room. The guards saw nothing. The Moroccans outside swear no one passed . . .'

'And El Aggahr?' demanded Cord. 'Who is he?'

'A jumped-up Mahhabi hill-thief, an enemy of justice, a—a political bandit.' It was Sharif who spoke, his voice again charged with anger. 'Who he is, what he is, I would give very much to know, Mr Cord. He appeared from nowhere just over a year ago. He has murdered, robbed, terrorised. We are a civilised people but I say this—when we get him, this El Aggahr will not die easily.'

'I'll believe you.' Cord glanced back at Maggie Delday. 'My package was delivered in Rabat early this morning. The one you got'—he shrugged—'well, he couldn't be in both places at once. How do you rate the house staff, captain?'

'All came with us from Jemma, the president's household staff,' said Sunner stiffly. 'Rule them out. They've too much to lose.'

'Or their families have?' queried Jackson cynically. 'What about your own men?'

'Handpicked.' The word snarled its indignation.

'For loyalty?' asked Maggie Delday sweetly. She looked past them towards the girl on the couch. 'Of course, you can buy most things, I suppose.'

Cord fought down a grin and turned back to Sharif. 'How many people know the programme ahead?'

'Only the few it concerns. Why?'

'Better keep it that way.' Cord signalled the others. 'We'd better leave now. That is, if you want me to take a proper interest in my work.'

Sharif nodded curtly. 'Do that, Mr Cord. My safety is at least partly in your hands. And if I die, plenty of others will follow—that is no threat, Mr Cord. It is simple fact.'

Sunner led them to the door. As they reached it, Cord looked back. The auburn-haired girl had crossed over to the window and was standing there. She saw him, deliberately ran a pink tongue-tip over her lips, then turned away.

'Bitch,' said Maggie Delday in a low, sharp voice.

He grinned and followed her out past the guard and down the corridor towards the car.

3

It seemed almost natural, strangely unalarming that someone should be firing an automatic rifle further along the valley. They emerged from the house and stopped on the verandah, listening while the crisp, staccato reports came in calm, regularly spaced bursts.

'Daily practice,' explained Captain Sunner. 'My fellows like to keep their hand in. We ration the ammunition, of course. It costs too much.'

'Everyone's economising this year,' said Talos Cord dryly, leaning back against the verandah rail. The station wagon was where they'd left it, but neither Roder nor the mercenary sergeant were in sight. 'Captain, I hate to sound sour. But President Sharif's schedule doesn't give us much time to be organised.'

'Sorry, but that's your problem,' shrugged Sunner with minimal sympathy. 'The schedule wasn't my idea, but he's right. The sooner Mohammed Sharif is back in Jemma, in direct control, the better for everyone.'

'You're still asking a lot,' said Maggie Delday quietly. While Jackson nodded agreement, she went on, 'Talos hasn't been here long enough to get his shoes dirty. He hasn't even seen our locations...'

The man shrugged again, hands in the side pockets of his dark blue battle blouse. 'I've been to both places, and I didn't see any particular difficulty. Give my squad a free hand and we'll take care of everything.'

Cord shook his head. 'U.N. installations are our responsibility. And you're forgetting Major Rucos. He has his own ideas on the situation.'

'Him?' Sunner didn't try to hide his dislike. 'I suppose we can't avoid the Moroccans being involved. That's inevitable and they've been fairly useful. But that doesn't change the rest. As the president's adviser I still demand the right of final approval.'

'If that's how you feel...' Cord sighed, looking across at the harsh, dark mountainside. Here and there stunted

46

patches of scrub clung among the rocks, reaching almost as high as the snowline.

Something glinted briefly up there. He watched for a moment, but it didn't happen again. It might have been sunlight on quartz. But he didn't think so.

'Well?' demanded Sunner.

'I think we'll go back inside,' said Cord quietly. 'I'm going to tell Sharif the visit is off—unless we get this settled right now.'

Sunner flushed. He met Cord's gaze angrily, started to speak, then fell silent. Cord didn't move, didn't speak. At last, the man swallowed the indignity of admitting defeat.

'At least I—ah—I should have the right to give an opinion on arrangements.'

'An opinion, yes.' Cord turned towards Jackson. 'Walt, could we get to the power station this afternoon?'

Jackson nodded. 'No problem, provided we skip lunch. You could see the place, then get to Marrakech before dusk. Joe Palombo and I roughed out some plans for the president's visit—basic protocol, that sort of thing. Maggie was re-drafting them. Right, Maggie?'

'They're ready,' she agreed. 'And Joe Palombo will probably be back at his office by then. You could finalise details with him.'

'That's the programme then.' Cord thumbed towards the car. 'Where's Roder?'

'Not far away,' said Sunner. He raised his voice. 'Sergeant . . . Sergeant Denke . . .'

A moment passed, then the tall, skeletal sergeant appeared from the nearest of the outhouses.

'Sir?'

'Mr Jackson's driver. Let him out now.'

Denke acknowledged with a wave and went back the

way he'd come. A low rumble of anger escaped from Jackson's lips.

'What do you mean, let him out?'

'One of our extra precautions.' Sunner smiled with a casual disinterest. 'All native civilians coming into the valley are—ah—being invited to wait in the duty hut.'

Jackson swore with a pungent, outback crudity then fell silent as, hands in his pockets, Roder made a nonchalant appearance from one of the huts. Sergeant Denke was close behind, a scowl on his flat-nosed face.

'Satisfied?' queried Sunner. Without waiting for an answer he switched his attention back to Cord. 'I'll be in Marrakech this evening. Why don't we meet then? It could be useful.'

Cord nodded. 'What time?'

'Before eight. I'll check with the UNESCO office when I reach town.'

Sunner stayed on the verandah as they went down to the station wagon. He gave a brief wave as Roder started up, then turned away.

.   .   .   .   .

No one said much until they left the valley and had checked out through the Moroccan army post. Then as the car began heading back down the mountain road, Maggie Delday gave a sigh.

'Well, you've seen it now. What do you think, Talos?'

'Of Sharif?' Cord relaxed back against the seat-cushions and gave a faint shake of his head. 'He's worried, but probably more angry than scared. I'm not sure about Sunner.'

'Stay that way,' advised Jackson abruptly. 'He's a polite brand of poison. Still'—the broad, red face split in

48

delighted recollection—'he backed down fast enough when you pressured him. What about you, Roder? Did they push you around much?'

'Me, boss?' The young Arab shook his head. 'I just do what I'm told. When the big *gamaagim* skull-face says move, I move.' His hands moved gently over the wheel, his face devoid of expression. 'He did not understand what I called him on the way back, but I think he guessed.'

Cord gave a soft chuckle of appreciation. 'What about the girl?'

'I imagined you'd get round to asking,' said Jackson slyly. 'You tell him, Maggie.'

'Apart from the obvious?' There was a cutting edge to the words. 'Her name is Mathilde Dolanne, she came with them, and she's part French, part Egyptian. She may have a typewriter along, but I've never heard her use it.'

'Maggie has a puritan streak deep down,' murmured Jackson. 'But Mathilde is quite a piece of furniture, and the rest is her business.' His stomach rumbled loudly and he grinned apologetically. 'Back there I said we could skip lunch. Maybe that wasn't such a good idea.' He waited hopefully, got no response, and sighed. 'Then at least we can pull in at a village somewhere and pick up some beer.'

They did, briefly, once they'd left the mountains behind. With the beer Roder managed a scrawny but well-cooked chicken, some native bread and a handful of oranges.

The car started off again. They ate as they travelled—and Jackson talked, using words like a thick paintbrush to outline life as he saw it.

'The world's crazy.' He smacked his artificial leg hard and cheerfully. 'I got this in North Africa, World War Two infantry style. Slowed me down too much for my old job, so I drifted into construction engineering. I studied and qualified, then land on the U.N. payroll. And where do they send me? Back to flaming North Africa!

'Morocco?' He shook his head. 'It's a tangle, Cord. A real tangle. Three out of four of the population can't read or write, yet they've a culture old enough to make Europe look mostly primitive. They're the kind of people who'll argue for hours over damn-all—then say "yes" when you least expect it. I still can't figure them.'

Geography, Jackson-style, was simple. Most of the north-west coastal strip was reasonably fertile and industry was beginning to build up in the few cities. But the rest was mountains, followed by wasteland desert, too much was a peasant economy balanced precariously near to poverty . . . which was where the UNESCO projects came in. The nuclear power plant would generate low-cost electricity for a new complex of chemical processing industries. Almost equally important, the power plant would be twinned with a desalination unit—a unit which would produce millions of gallons of fresh water daily from the sea, fresh water at practically zero cost.

'They can pipe it inland for irrigation.' Jackson took a long, thankful swig from his bottle of beer. 'Most things out here depend on irrigation—me included.'

'And it's a lot worse in an oven like the Arabian Peninsula,' said Cord softly. 'No wonder Sharif wants to see the plant before he goes home. If he wins one for Jemma he'll rate as a hero. What would you say, Roder?'

Their driver shrugged non-committally. 'Maybe that is what he wants, Mr Cord.' He hunched a little lower over the wheel, taking the station wagon round a corner something close to a four-wheel drift.

'For the love of . . .' Jackson spluttered and brushed

spilled beer from his jacket as the tyre-scream died. 'Take it easy, you mad basket!' He sighed, then returned to his subject. 'The soil erosion deal is another good one for him. Right, Maggie?'

She nodded agreement. 'Probably, though it is a lot less spectacular. It's more a survey and teaching job, backing up local effort. Hill terracing, fencing—showing villagers what to do. They've made quite a piece of progress at the Takenakht site. I was up there last week.'

'Interested in it?' queried Cord. 'I thought you were purely on the administrative side.'

'I just go up there sometimes.' The words came almost curtly. Her lips tightened a little, then she firmly changed the subject. 'This man El Aggahr—do you really think he'll try something?'

'He's making it look that way,' said Cord soberly. 'And he gets around. I've a feeling there was someone back on that mountain, watching our little visit. Don't ask me what's liable to happen. He's the one that's setting the pace.'

He pulled one of the yellow-leafed cheroots from his top pocket and felt for a match.

No, other people had to make the moves for the moment. He could only wait, be ready for the obvious, search for the unexpected—and hope he could find it before time ran out.

Insulated within the vehicle's steel and glass, occasionally jolted as the high-sprung suspension took a pothole, he settled back to watch the flat, level monotony slip by.

.   .   .   .   .

Enveena Nuclear Generating Station was located near Cap Cantin, on the edge of a low rock escarpment overlooking the almost painfully deep blue of the Atlantic.

51

It was close to mid-afternoon when they reached the site, a raw confusion of chewed-up ground, half-completed buildings and tangled, apparently endless pipework.

A high fence, barbed-wire topped, ran round the perimeter. Inside, heavy equipment filled the air with its mechanical din and the smell of diesel exhausts. Most of the Arab labour, sweat glistening on their bodies, worked stripped to ragged shorts and torn singlets.

A heavy truck passed through the only gate just ahead of them. Then, with a wave to the waiting guard, Roder swung the station wagon into the half-completed maze, bumped through it with an easy familiarity, and finally stopped outside a long wooden hut.

They got out, Jackson cursing as he massaged a cramp from his good leg.

'Half an hour should do it, Roder.' He glanced questioningly at the girl. 'Want to come along, Maggie?'

She shook her head. 'While I'm here I might as well see the stores invoice clerk—it'll save me a trip later.'

They watched her go. Then, as Roder wandered off on some errand of his own, Jackson cleared his throat.

'Cord, maybe I should have told you about Maggie. You saw how she dried up when we mentioned the erosion scheme?'

'I wondered.' Cord watched a man on a latticework of steel scaffolding above them. Carrying a length of timber, he moved from one section to another with catlike agility.

'That's where her husband worked. Harry Delday was some kind of soil technologist—wasn't out long. I only met him a couple of times.' Jackson rasped a thumb along his chin then shrugged. 'He was driving into Marrakech one night, coming down from the mountains. They didn't find him till the next morning. The car was at the bottom of a gully, with Harry pinned underneath. He died just before they got him out.'

'And Maggie?'

'She came out for the funeral, stayed on and—well, started working for us. I thought maybe it would help to know.'

It did. He nodded his thanks and Jackson looked relieved.

'Right, then suppose we take a look around.'

The tour didn't take long. The generating station's lay-out stretched to the edge of the low cliffs, and down below long lines of heavy concrete piping already emerged from the creaming breakers to a series of half-completed pump-houses. From the pump-houses, other pipes came up to the main station.

'Satisfied?' queried Jackson at last.

'I've seen what I want,' qualified Cord. 'Now I'd like a layout plan.'

'We've got something better.' Grinning, Jackson set a fast, limping pace towards another of the long, wooden huts. He plunged through a door and led the way into an inner office. A bushy-haired man in shirt-sleeves looked up from his desk and gave a nod of recognition.

'This is Tom Fielden, the nearest thing we've got to a site agent.' Jackson completed the introductions with a minimum of formality. 'Tom, let him see Tiny Town.'

Fielden, a lanky figure, uncurled from behind the desk, beckoned them to follow, and guided them through still another door. The next office was entirely occupied by a billiard-table size model of how the completed station would look, complete in detail down to a row of toy cars in a white-lined parking lot.

'We'll bring President Sharif here tomorrow, right at the start,' said Jackson. 'This really tells the story—I can't see him being keen about the mess outside.'

'You said tomorrow?' The site agent's mouth stayed open, his eyes showed worry.

'That's what he just decided,' nodded Cord. 'Why? Any particular problem?'

'Plenty of them.' Fielden scratched his head. 'Apart from anything else this means I've a site to tidy, a tour programme to organise, an office to clean up so they can finish with tea and buns . . .'

'Details,' grunted Jackson with scant sympathy.

Cord ignored them for a moment, looking at the model, translating it back into half-finished terms.

'Tell me about the desalination plant,' he said suddenly.

'You could call it a big kettle, or a whole row of them,' said Fielden. He stopped, frowning for simplicities. 'We'll use the waste heat from the secondary cooler tubes round the reactor core. Pump that heat under kettles full of sea water, bring them to the boil, trap the steam, condense it, and you've a continuous flow of distilled water.'

'Which tastes like hell,' commented Jackson.

Fielden grinned, at home with his subject. 'So we add a dash of straight sea water as flavouring.

'The one flow of waste heat is enough right down the line, because water will boil at progressively lower temperatures if you reduce atmospheric pressure. Each kettle works within a lower pressure—and we are planning an output of seventy million gallons a day.'

'That's what President Sharif will want to hear,' said Cord, walking slowly round the model. 'I'm more interested in that guard-fence on the perimeter. Is it patrolled by night?'

54

'Always,' confirmed Fielden. 'We've three night men, each with a dog. There's another man on duty at the gate. We need them. The locals have taking ways—they'd grab anything that wasn't nailed down.'

'You're weak down here.' Cord stabbed a finger at the seaward side. 'A man could swim round the end of the wire and come ashore. If he was a man with a rifle, and he got in among the construction work, how long till you'd find him?'

Fielden shook his head. 'Probably we wouldn't, not in that tangle. What can we do about it?'

'Raise a few extra men, men you can trust. Can you rig some lights for tonight?' The man's slow, positive nod satisfied Cord and he went on. 'Double your usual fence patrols. Light up where you can, and especially along the shore. Have a permanent watch there. Tomorrow'—he pursed his lips for a moment—'tomorrow the work gangs offer a potential risk. Give them the day off.'

'With pay?' queried Jackson sharply. 'Joe Palombo is the only one who can authorise that. And he won't like the idea.'

'I'm authorising it. And the cost.' Wryly, he wondered how Andrew Beck was going to react to that little item when it got round to the inter-departmental memo stage. 'Organise President Sharif's programme so that he's out in the open as little as possible. He'll arrive in the afternoon—you'll get the exact time later, and I'll be back before then.' He glanced at each man in turn. 'The Moroccans have the job of getting him here in one piece, which is Major Rucos's worry. But once Sharif drives through that gate he's our responsibility.'

'Happy thought,' murmured Jackson sardonically.

They left Fielden still worrying and scratching his head. Cord knew just how he felt.

. . . . .

Maggie Delday was back in the station wagon, Roder near at hand, when they emerged from the hut. The bustle of construction work hadn't slowed, the machinery was as noisy as ever.

'You.' Jackson stopped the Arab as he moved to open the passenger door. 'You take things easier on the run back. Right?'

'Okay, Mr Jackson.' A grin slipped Roder's face. 'I just like the hurry-hurry.'

'And I know where you learned it,' grumbled Jackson, heaving himself aboard. 'That damned oil-drilling outfit you were with. That's where he came from, Cord— walked in out of nowhere, talking broken Brooklyn. Tell him how far you walked, Roder.'

'Four days,' said Roder casually. 'They were okay, the *amrikki*. But a man should not stay still.' He paused, a strangely guarded interest in his eyes. 'Of what people are you, Mr Cord? Sometimes you sound *inglizzi*, sometimes not.'

Cord shook his head. 'I've no particular label, Roder.'

'Oh.' Puzzled, Roder fell silent. Without further comment he watched Cord get aboard then went round and started up.

They talked briefly on the way. The road was straight and fast, the villages still few but larger. Some had electricity and filling stations, though the butcher shop could be a tree with a carcass hung from a branch, flies swarming, the proprietor squatting beneath with the knives of his trade spread on the ground.

56

And everywhere there were people. People walking, resting, riding overloaded donkeys or an occasional camel. People in native robes, European cast-offs or a mixture of both. People who seemed busy heading from nowhere to nowhere. He'd never seen so many beings on the move without apparent aim or purpose.

'You see them all over,' nodded Maggie Delday when he asked. 'Some visiting, shopping, going home from work—miles don't matter much to them. But the rest—they're just natural nomads, people travelling.'

Her eyes stayed on his face then, quickly, almost apologetically she glanced away. Wondering about the scar, he guessed.

'It takes all kinds, I suppose.' The words were trite and annoyed him as he sat back.

But it did. Here he was with a cheerful, one-legged Australian, a drifting, chain-smoking Arab, and a fair-haired widow who probably wasn't aware she was struggling to keep a last link with the past. And he made a good fourth.

The scar. Most people made it obvious they'd like to ask about it. Few did.

His left hand came up, touching the line with the gentle familiarity of an old friend. The scar, the past and Andrew Beck. They were all bound close together, added up to a scrawny eight-year-old boy salvaged from a civilian internment camp in Shanghai after the Japs surrendered.

Andrew Beck had arrived as a visiting Allied officer and found him there. A kid who couldn't remember anything before the camp, who'd been handed in on his own when that scar was still an open wound, the only identification the fact that his ragged shirt had 'P. Cord' sewn neatly into the neckband.

57

It was Beck who combed the records and learned that a British family named Cord had been aboard a cargo ship believed sunk without survivors as it tried to escape from a beleaguered Hong Kong. Beck who practically smuggled Peter Cord, orphan, no known relatives, out of camp. To re-christen him Talos and adopt him as his own.

But not for the ordinary reasons. Cord smiled wryly as the car slowed briefly for a junction.

Talos.

The Cretan myth had become a nightly story. How the ancient King Minos had possessed a giant bronze robot of that name, a robot which endlessly patrolled the shores of his island kingdom. Untiring, faithful, incorruptible, fire spouting from its mouth, the bronze Talos maintained law and order—and chased off unwanted visitors, including a wild character called Jason who was on the prowl for a Golden Fleece.

Andrew Beck had had it planned even before Field Reconnaissance existed. By training, by conditioning, he'd set out to create his own robot, create a man insulated against all outside pressures, reared to regard the world as his family tree.

The experiment hadn't quite succeeded. Maybe the same thing could be said about the U.N., though it would have to do its shaky best until something more effectual came along. Too often Talos Cord realised only too well he was flesh and blood, too often Beck failed to recognise the signs.

But even that old-time robot had had its troubles. And it had been wrecked when a woman managed to drain the life-fluid from that bronze bulk.

There was always a woman around.

Like Maggie Delday. Or that auburn-haired package Mathilde. Put together, he'd a feeling they'd scrap like alley-cats.

He wondered what Beck would have said about them. If anything.

.   .   .   .   .

Half of Marrakech is crowded, noisy old-quarter Arab. The rest is wide avenues, fountains and twentieth century European. You can live in one half without needing to know the other exists.

UNESCO project headquarters was in the new sector, a white, flat-roofed building on the edge of the business area. The station wagon stopped outside, Jackson left them briefly, then emerged from the building again in a matter of minutes. Shaking his head, he opened the rear door and looked in.

'No word of Joe Palombo yet,' he reported. 'Looks like he's having a long session with those civil servants, and most of our place is starting to close up for the night.'

Cord glanced at his watch. It was leaving five p.m. 'Then what's the programme? If Sunner is coming in . . .'

'Let him wait,' said Jackson airily. 'Anyway, I'll hang on here for a spell. Maggie, you take him to the hotel, get him booked in. I'll come along later. Okay?'

They nodded. Jackson closed the door, gave a parting grin, and headed away.

'The Affri, Roder.' Maggie Delday turned to Cord as the car started off again. 'Most of us live there. We qualify for off-season rates.'

'Sounds fine.' Anything did. He was tired of travel, his shirt felt sticky with perspiration, any kind of a break would be welcome.

The hotel was a couple of minutes drive distant. Set in its own wooded grounds, the Affri was a tall blend of reinforced concrete and Moroccan traditional and as they stopped at the main door Roder nipped out with unusual speed.

'*Tariiq* . . . leave us.' He brushed aside the fez-topped doorman, took Cord's travel bag, and followed stubbornly at their heels into the cool, mosaic-tiled lobby. Cord registered at the desk, took his room key, then turned.

'All set. Any plans ahead, Maggie?'

She shook her head. 'Freshen up slowly, I suppose. Then I'll think about a drink and a meal.'

'Like to join me?'

'All right,' she agreed, a faint twinkle in her eyes. 'But I warn you, I eat a lot.'

'It doesn't show,' he assured her. 'What time?'

'Around seven. There's a bar beside the restaurant. I'll be there.' She smiled again and left him.

.   .   .   .   .

Cord's room was on the second floor. Roder still trailing, he reached it, opened the door and took a look around. A large French window led onto a pocket-sized sun balcony, a bathroom and shower were located off one corner, and the rest seemed reasonable.

'Fine.' He glanced at Roder. 'Dump the bag anywhere, and thanks.'

Nodding, Roder laid the travel grip on the bed then hesitated. 'Mr Cord . . .'

'I know.' Nodding, Cord reached into his pockets.

'*Laa* . . . no, Mr Cord. Not money.' Indignantly, Roder drew himself upright. 'I wish to ask something, please.'

'Then go ahead,' invited Cord, sprawling back on the

bed with a sigh of relief. 'What's the problem?'

'This President Sharif'—the thin, pock-marked face twisted in an awkward grin—'you like him?'

'Does anyone?' parried Cord lazily. 'No, not much. But I don't need to. I'm paid to do a job, just like you. Why?'

'*Wala haage* . . . nothing.' Roder scratched his chest under the shirt in self-conscious style. 'Except that I have heard some strange things here in the *suk*, the old town. There are people who say maybe this El Aggahr is not the one to fear.'

'What people?' Cord levered himself up on his elbows, immediately interested. 'Let's have it, Roder. I want to hear the rest.'

'Just people—they gossip in the markets.' Roder sucked his cheeks for a moment then, eyes watchful, began to edge back towards the door. 'Mr Cord, it would be a bad thing if you guarded against the wrong danger.'

Cord sat up, making it unhurried, more and more conscious that behind the stumbling words lay something more than this thin, wiry figure was prepared to spell out. 'Don't try to scare me with shadows,' he said softly. 'Who else would want Sharif out of the way?'

Roder shook his head. 'You are the one who must find out. I only tell what I hear.' Suddenly, the old, insolent grin slipped back into place. 'Have one damn fine night, Mr Cord.'

He had gone before Cord could speak again.

As the door closed Cord stayed where he was, his lips pursed thoughtfully. What Roder had told him was one thing, why he'd told him another. At last he sighed, rolled off the bed in a cat-like move which brought him to his feet, and reached for his travel bag.

A shave, a shower and some shut-eye. There were

other variations on the 'three sh . . .' theme, but that one would do him. He opened the travel bag, found what he wanted, and grinned wryly in the process.

Somewhere along the line the bag had been searched—neatly, systematically, with a good attempt at exact replacement. The simple zip lock hadn't been damaged. It was simple for exactly that reason. Make it easier for the professional and you didn't end up needing a new bag.

The small black metal box lay halfway down. Inside was a Swiss Neuhausen automatic and six clips of fat, glistening 9 mm Parabellum cartridges. Cord checked the gun, fed in a clip, then returned gun and box. Field Reconnaissance's code was that there was something slightly incongruous about a peacemaker with a gun—until it was needed.

For the moment, a clean shirt and his shaving kit mattered more. Cord located them, stripped happily, and headed for the bathroom.

Fifteen minutes later, feeling human again, his short black hair and muscular body still glistening wet from the shower, he padded back into the bedroom still rubbing himself down with a towel.

'Good evening, Mr Cord,' said a dry, sardonic voice. 'You sang quite loudly in there.'

Cord looked, grinned, and rubbed on. Major Rucos was sprawled back in a chair, uniform tunic unfastened, swagger stick and green beret lying to one side. The Moroccan security man reached out and lazily threw him the clean shirt.

'Thanks.' Cord pulled it on and jerked his head towards the door. 'Pass-key?'

Rucos spread his small, thin hands. 'I felt sure you would not object.'

'And it wouldn't matter a damn if I did.' Cord continued dressing, taking his time. 'Social call, major?'

'No.' Rucos produced his cigarettes, then, as Cord shook his head, lit one using a holder. 'I thought you might be interested in the little we have learned about the microphone at Rabat. It was retrieved this afternoon.' A grimace twisted his immaculate moustache-line. 'Unfortunately, it happened just after someone started a small fire in a nearby office. In the confusion . . .'

'It went.' Cord nodded his understanding. 'You came a long way to tell me. Or is there more, major? About El Aggahr, for instance?'

'That one?' The bright blue eyes flickered away for a moment. 'You have been researching quickly, Mr Cord. But *irragel feen* . . . where is the man? All we have are stories. No, my problem is your problem, Mr Cord—this programme President Sharif has been unwise enough to plan. We received details in Rabat this morning.' Rucos drew unhappily on the cigarette and let the smoke out slowly, thoughtfully. 'I do not like it. It makes me uneasy.'

'Join the club,' invited Cord, shoving his feet into the waiting moccasins. 'I've met Sharif and seen the nuclear plant. Neither of them fills me with mad-gay delight.'

The Moroccan puzzled over the words for a moment then nodded his understanding. 'And the red-faced Captain Sunner?' he asked softly. 'You found him capable?'

'I found him too sure of himself.' Finished, Cord perched on the edge of the bed. 'But that's a tough-looking little outfit he has up there.'

'Tough and brutal.' Rucos's face tightened. 'They shot a shepherd dead last week. The man had wandered past our own guards somehow. Sunner's men did not wait to question him.' He shook his head slowly, almost forlornly.

'My government believes in Pan-Arab unity. That is one reason why our invitation went to Jemma when President Sharif was ill. But we did not expect what arrived.'

'Sunner's coming in tonight,' volunteered Cord. 'He wants to talk about tomorrow's arrangements.'

'In which I hope he will play little part,' grated Rucos grimly. 'Anyway, he has other business here. The Europeans in which President Sharif is so interested, business men of some kind, are staying in this hotel.'

'They've arrived?' Cord raised a surprised eyebrow.

'Two days ago. Four men—their passports say they are Greek, their business interests are uncertain, but they have money. So far only Captain Sunner has spoken to them, handling preliminaries.' A sudden frown crossed Rucos's face and switched away from the topic. 'Mr Cord, that "contact" you mentioned back at the airport, the hope that tonight...'

'I told you,' reminded Cord wearily. 'It was a bluff.'

'Very well.' Rucos sounded far from convinced. 'Then let us talk about tomorrow. There are problems.'

They got down to detail. Two things were quickly established in Cord's mind. The Moroccan was a professional who knew the ambush and attack trade—which was reasonable, remembering it had once been his own. Soothe that Berber pride when it appeared, and they could plan together. Rucos's worries were part protocol, even to terms of which flag would fly highest, and part practical. But at last they had the final arrangements. Route security and outside guards were completely Moroccan responsibility. The guard inside the wire fence would be a shared task.

'That leaves Sunner's men,' said Cord, sitting back and reaching for a cheroot. 'What do we do with them?'

'I know what I would like to do,' murmured Rucos with a rare sparkle of icy humour. 'In the old days'—he shrugged almost regretfully—'*khalas* that time is finished. But there must be no incidents.'

'Sunner and maybe a couple more of them will have to be with Sharif on the tour,' mused Cord. 'But if I find a spare corner somewhere and a few crates of beer that should keep the rest occupied.'

'Good.' Fastening his tunic, Rucos got to his feet. 'Allah willing, all will go well. If not, we have done our best.'

'And your bosses will see it that way?' asked Cord lazily.

'No.' Rucos reached the door, opened it, then gave a wry smile. 'Would yours, Mr Cord?'

He left. Alone again, Cord lit the cheroot and switched on the bedside radio. Fiddling briefly with the knobs, he picked up a British news broadcast. The first few words made it clear the world was in its usual battered state.

He glanced at his watch, decided it was time to head down in search of Maggie, and switched off the newscaster in mid-sentence.

Talos Cord had enough troubles of his own.

4

Maggie Delday admitted to herself she was 'tarted up' with more than usual care. She hadn't got round to admitting why.

But her short, fair hair was brushed back till it shone. From near the rear of her wardrobe she'd brought out a pastel green linen shift with a low square-cut neck and fractional sleeves. Conscious of her height, she'd settled for a pair of low-heeled, backless slippers, gold embroidered, which had been the subject of a week's bargaining in the *suk*. The rest was a light make-up job and a carefully measured amount of a Balmain perfume Palombo and Walt Jackson had given her at Christmas.

Cord found her perched on a stool at the far corner of the Affri bar. It was a chrome and mirrors place where a tepid central fountain and a surround of potted cactus constituted the beginning and end of atmosphere. He looked her over with deliberate care and then gave a soft, appreciative whistle.

'Nice, Maggie—very nice,' he approved, sliding onto the next stool. 'Give me a moment to get used to it.'

She laughed, pleased and amused. 'I get sick of those damned shirts and slacks. But they're practical for most of the time.'

'I prefer the non-practical.' She was drinking vodka and lemon. Cord ordered another and a long whisky sour for himself. Then he eased round on the stool, looking across the half-filled tables.

'Expecting someone?' she queried.

'This business quartet who're going to see Sharif. Major Rucos looked in—he says they're staying here. Greeks bringing money.'

Maggie Delday shook her head. 'Sorry, I can't help. But I've a message for you from Walt Jackson. He 'phoned. Joe Palombo missed the 'plane, but he's driving back. The message is Joe must see you tonight, but it'll be late on.'

'That kind of popularity I can do without,' he declared wryly. The drinks arrived. He paid for them, took a long taste of his own, and drew a deep, satisfied breath.

'Maggie, tell me something. How long has Roder been on the payroll?'

'A few weeks. Why?'

He shrugged easily. 'Curiosity mainly,' he lied. 'When I'm a passenger I like to know whose foot will hit the brake pedal—if he knows there's such a thing. What happened to the man before him?'

'He walked out on us. They do that sometimes.' Her mouth shaped doubtfully. 'No other reason?'

'None.' He gave her a cigarette and lit it. 'Walt told me about your husband, Maggie. It must have been a bad time. But—well, you weren't out here before it happened. Why stay now?'

'I don't know.' She nursed the fresh glass between both hands, the cigarette smouldering beside her. 'We'd only been married a couple of years, no family, and I still had a job back in Edinburgh—I was in an accountant's office. But after it happened I just didn't want to go back to that.'

'You like the life?'

'It's different.' For a moment Maggie Delday seemed to have forgotten him then she took a sip from her drink and smiled. 'What about you? Walt says Field Reconnaissance come close to cloak-and-dagger stuff.'

'That's one view. We're more like so many little fire extinguishers—stopping things reaching the stage where the big fire brigades are needed. We like to call ourselves peacemakers.' It was true, except that they were the kind of peacemakers who sometimes had to get down to pretty bloody business in the process. 'When should we eat?'

'Any time. The house speciality is *mechoui*—that's spit-roasted sheep.' She stopped, looking past him, her face tightening a little. 'I think your Greeks have arrived with company.'

67

He'd guessed what to expect even before he turned.

Captain Sunner led the party coming into the bar. He was out of uniform, Mathilde Dolanne by his side, a quartet of dark-suited middle-aged men trailing self-consciously a few steps behind. The Greeks—if Rucos was right on that—were wooden-faced, sharp-eyed little men who at first glance seemed almost identical.

But, inevitably, Mathilde was the magnet attracting attention from every table. That long, auburn hair, plaited into a single braid, was pinned high on her head by a jewelled comb. Under a loose grey gaberdine version of a Bedouin woman's robe, worn open, the hood thrown back, she wore a high-collared full-length kaftan in peach silk. It had a black key pattern embroidered heavily along the hem.

Sunner settled his party at a table in the far corner, Mathilde on his right, and signalled a waiter.

Cord ran a thoughtful, wary hand along his chin. 'If I go over for a minute or so I can get rid of Sunner for the evening.'

'That's a good enough reason,' agreed Maggie Delday, a slight chill behind the words. 'Do you need a better?'

He grinned. 'Come off it, Maggie. I'm not sticking my neck out in any other direction.'

'Then go ahead.' She found a sudden interest in reading the bottle labels behind the bar. 'It's your neck, anyway.'

Still grinning, he slipped down from the stool and made a leisurely way to Sunner's table.

'Hello, Cord.' Sunner's stained teeth showed in brief, friendly fashion. 'I planned to look you up. Now you're here, pull up another chair.'

'Thanks, but I've got company.' Cord met the girl's calm, interested gaze. 'Nice to see you along, Mathilde.'

'Much more of that mountain and I would probably go mad,' she said in lazy, matter-of-fact fashion. 'At least, this makes a change.'

Hastily, Sunner cleared his throat. 'Cord, you'd better meet my guests.' He turned to the Greeks. 'Mr Cord is from the U.N. He is helping plan—ah—arrangements.'

Introduced one by one, the quartet had limp handshakes and disinterested expressions—all except their leader, a bald, thickset man named Pauol. He nodded a curt greeting then asked in blunt, accented English, 'How likely is it someone will try to kill President Sharif?'

'It's possible, but we don't plan on letting it happen,' countered Cord.

'Nor does President Sharif,' said Mathilde silkily. 'Ask Captain Sunner.'

Sunner scowled unhappily. 'We're taking all precautions. Any new difficulties so far, Cord?'

Cord shook his head. 'I've talked to Major Rucos. He'll liase with you on route security tomorrow, and the Moroccan army will operate a joint guard with my people inside the power plant area. That'll leave you to provide a couple of personal guards for Sharif during the actual tour. Any other men you bring along can stay in reserve.'

The red, fleshy face didn't show particular approval. But Sunner didn't argue. 'All right. I'm planning a two o'clock arrival. And we'll have an additional member in the party. Abdul Zieull is flying in tomorrow, first thing. He's our Minister for Internal Affairs—there's been a flare-up in Jemma over the Wat Said killing, and the president wants a first-hand report.'

'We'll cope,' nodded Cord. 'You'll be along, Mathilde?'

'I wouldn't miss it,' she said sardonically, slipping the robe from her shoulders and over the back of her chair.

'I love power stations.'

Sunner forced a smile. 'Mathilde and I are staying here overnight. Then we'll meet Zieull at the airstrip in the morning.'

'You'd better let Rucos know.' Still curious, Cord switched his attention back to the silent Greeks. 'President Sharif mentioned he was meeting you this week. What's involved—investment projects?'

'Among other things,' answered Pauol shortly. He glanced at his companions and spoke quickly. They grinned. One of them laughed outright. Pauol shook his head quickly. 'Our apologies, Mr Cord. You could say that, like your UNESCO, we hope to make some changes in Jemma—and of course, some income for ourselves. There have been some interesting geological surveys out there, with new results.'

'Oil?' Cord raised a surprised eyebrow.

'They import every barrel. No, we are interested in certain mineral deposits. We are—ah—in delicate negotiation for exclusive rights. You understand?'

'I hope somebody does, because I don't know what's going on,' said Mathilde wearily. 'What happened to those drinks we ordered? Never mind—I'll find out for myself.' She rose, her eyes on Cord. 'Suppose I go over with you and say hello to Mrs Delday?'

'She'd like that,' said Cord mildly, keeping his face straight.

A hand resting lightly on his arm, her perfumed body close, she let him lead her over. Maggie Delday was waiting with a thin-lipped smile.

'Hello, Mathilde.' Her eyes flickered icily over the dress. 'Very nice. Who chose it for you?'

The other girl didn't bat an eyelid. One slim, tanned

hand made a brief, deprecating gesture. 'You always amuse me, Maggie. But yes, it was a present. An appreciation from President Sharif.'

'I'm sure you earned it,' said Maggie Delday dryly.

'I try.' Mathilde's mouth shaped a pout. 'I've never seen you in a dress before. Don't you find it—well, strange? I think of you more as something different.'

Duel or skirmish, Cord decided if this was a social call he wouldn't want to be around if they ever became earnest. But Mathilde was already beginning to drift away.

'Look after her, Mr Cord,' she advised sweetly. 'I like seeing people enjoying themselves, and Mrs Delday gets so few opportunities.'

She left, and Maggie Delday swore softly under her breath.

'Why the feud?' queried Cord, holding back a grin. 'Because she's with Sharif?'

'If she wants to trollop, that's her business.' Maggie pushed her empty glass aside and refused another. 'Some people just dislike each other on sight. We're two of them.' She grimaced, as if getting rid of a minor unpleasantness. 'I'm hungry.'

They ate at a window table in the restaurant, which had a through way to the Affri's casino—a notice above the gambling hall door warned that entry was forbidden to Muslims, juveniles and armed forces in uniform, but that didn't seem to slow business.

Cord was more interested in what lay outside, beyond the window. Water glinting in the wavering moonlight, the swimming pool was separated from the hotel by a broad stretch of patio. On the other side, a row of changing cubicles backed onto an ornamental garden, the shrubs and bushes vague outlines in the night.

71

'It's heated—the pool, I mean,' volunteered Maggie Delday. 'Not many people use it this late.'

'Which seems a waste.' He eyed her speculatively. 'What do you think?'

'Now?' She started to frown then gave a small nod instead. 'Well, I've a swimsuit upstairs. You?'

He nodded, and signalled for a bill.

.   .   .   .   .

The North African night was chill, a low wind murmuring through the leaves of the shrubs around. But the water in the pool was kept around eighty degrees—like a warm kiss, decided Cord as he dived then came up spluttering near the middle.

He floated, waiting, as Maggie emerged from a changing box. Her swimsuit was one-piece, dark blue and simply cut. She stopped, toes on the edge of the pool, then entered in a forward half-roll which left scarcely a ripple as she vanished. Brief seconds passed, then she reappeared beside him.

'All right?' She brushed her hair back with one hand, grinning like a schoolgirl in the moonlight.

'Couldn't be better.' Cord tried a few experimental backstrokes, then floated again and was content to watch her. She moved well, smoothly, her body capturing a new, lithe beauty in the process. Then she came back, talked him into racing a length, and it took an effort to keep up with the fast crawl-stroke she produced out of nowhere.

'Enough.' Breathing heavily, he sat on the edge for a moment then got to his feet and helped her up beside him. She seemed to shiver a little at the grip on her arm, then smiled.

'I'll freeze like this.'

'Uh-huh.' He looked at her for a moment longer then realised she really was shivering. 'Come on then.'

They went back towards the changing boxes, flimsy, three-quarter door affairs, dark in the shadows. She reached the one she'd used, opened the door then suddenly, wordlessly, held out her hand.

He took it and followed her in. When he kissed her, gently at first then hard, searching, demanding, she gave a soft sound deep in her throat. Then they were locked together, the scent of her body sharp in his nostrils, the rumple of a towel their pillow, the world a clinging, fast-breathing hunger then a sigh.

.   .   .   .   .

'Don't you want to know why?'

She asked it in almost childish fashion as he lit a cigarette and placed it between her lips.

'Should I?' He shook his head. 'That might spoil it, Maggie.'

'Maybe. I'—the cigarette glowed brighter for an instant—'I don't know. I don't think I care, anyway.'

Suddenly she moved away from him. He heard soft, rustling noises in the darkness.

'What the hell are you doing?' he demanded lazily.

'Getting dressed,' she said briskly. 'I'm still freezing—and you've got Joe Palombo coming over, remember?'

'I remember.' He shook his head and chuckled.

'What's so funny?'

'Nothing, Maggie,' he said softly. 'Nothing that matters. You're right. We'd better move. I wouldn't want to keep your boss waiting.'

His wristwatch said ten thirty as they looked in at the Affri's bar. There was no sign of either Walt Jackson or

73

Palombo, and Sunner's party had gone.

'He'll be,' declared Maggie positively. She fought back the beginnings of a yawn and considered him almost shyly. 'But I think I'd better call it a day, Talos. I had a pretty early start.' Her mouth kept a smile under control. 'And a fairly hectic finish.'

Her room was on the third floor. Cord went with her on the elevator. She stopped him coming out as the door opened.

'Joe Palombo, I know.'

She nodded, kissed him quickly, her hand running gently over the scar on his cheek. Then she stepped back and the elevator doors closed.

Cord went down to the floor below, walked to his room, opened the door, and was reaching for the light switch when he stopped, sniffing the strange tobacco smoke in the air.

'Easy,' said a crisp voice with a strong American accent. 'It's only me—Palombo.'

He relaxed, switched on the light, and a tall, slightly-built man, youngish, with spectacles, prematurely grey hair, and a rather tired smile rose from the chair beside the bed.

'Sorry, Cord.' Joe Palombo blinked sheepishly. I looked around, couldn't find you, and felt damned near bushed—so I got a floor waiter to let me in. You had to get back here sometime.' He paused as Cord tossed wet trunks and towel on the floor. 'I heard you were with Maggie. Swimming?'

'Yes.' It was cold in the room. Cord found the heating regulator and flicked it up a few notches. The curtains hadn't been closed, but the balcony window was shut. 'How did you make out at Rabat?'

'That?' Palombo dismissed the matter with a shake of his head. 'Just a routine tussle. No, I had to see you about this Sharif business. I talked to Walt. What you've done about tomorrow seems fine, but . . .' he stopped, gnawing lightly on his lower lip.

'It's not perfect, if that's what you mean,' admitted Cord.

'It's Sharif himself who worries me.' Palombo frowned. 'I picked up a hint from—well, someone fairly high up in Rabat. Just a hint, that we should take a closer look at what's going on before any aid agreements are signed.'

'Meaning?' Cord crossed to the window, looking out at the night.

'I don't know. I'm a project administrator who feels out of his depth.' Palombo fumbled in an inside pocket and dragged out an envelope. 'Maybe this will help. It was radioed to our local operator about an hour ago, origin New York.' He grimaced ruefully. 'I can't make sense of it, but you'll know your own damned code.'

He came over, holding the envelope.

Next instant the window glass erupted inward in a staccato hammer of gunfire, flying splinters and whining ricochets. Something hot and angry raked across Cord's arm as he made a desperate bid to throw himself clear. Something else tore against his side.

He hit the floor, rolling. Palombo was still crumpling, mouth open in soundless surprise, folding like an abandoned puppet. The man collapsed across the bed—and another long burst of fire raked the room. Furniture splintered, slugs tore a crazy pattern across the opposite wall.

Then it stopped.

A woman was screaming somewhere. There were

shouts in the corridor. Cord crawled towards the light switch, arm stinging, his side aching. He killed the light then went back through the sudden gloom to Palombo's limp figure. The project director lay face down, the coverlet already stickily wet with blood.

Gently, Cord eased the man round. Palombo had been hit twice in the chest but was still breathing. Cord cursed, remembering the warning he'd handed out to Sharif about windows, remembering other things.

Fists began beating on the room door. Keeping low, he drew the curtains shut before he crossed over and switched the light on again. The envelope with the radio message was lying on the floor, near the bed. He tucked it in his pocket. The fists beat more urgently on the door then, suddenly, it opened.

'M'sieu Cord . . .' backed by a couple of porters and assorted guests the Affri's night manager, a pale-faced European, looked past him at the shambles and swallowed hard.

'We need a doctor and an ambulance,' said Cord in a weary, colourless voice. 'Make it quick—unless you want a man to die.'

The night manager stared for a moment longer then reacted. A barked instruction, and the nearest porter set off at a run.

.   .   .   .   .

Time telescoped. A couple of uniformed gendarmes were first to arrive, then a doctor, a young Frenchman with a crew-cut who'd been at the downstairs roulette tables. He said nothing, humming grimly under his breath as he worked on Palombo.

Cord waited, tight-lipped. Even if he'd wanted to leave

the gendarmes at the door didn't appear amenable. Then a fresh bustle in the corridor heralded two Red Crescent ambulance men with a stretcher, Major Rucos and Walt Jackson at their heels.

'Any luck outside?' asked Cord with little hope.

'My men are still searching.' Rucos watched Palombo's limp figure transferred to the stretcher then, as the ambulance men prepared to leave he stepped forward. '*Duktuur?*'

'*Hamdaan* . . . he's weak.' The crew-cut head shook soberly. 'He may live, he may not. One bullet is near the heart—it will depend on surgery.'

'I—I'd better go with him,' decided Jackson, watching the stretcher leave.

'Go ahead,' agreed Cord wearily. 'Keep in touch.'

Jackson limped out, his face strained and worried. A nod from Rucos, and one of the gendarmes followed.

'Now, m'sieu . . .' the doctor beckoned Cord towards a chair. He went over and sat down, wincing as his blood-stained jacket and shirt were peeled off. Major Rucos stood over them, the swagger stick tapping impatiently against his leg.

'We can talk while he works,' exploded Rucos suddenly. The doctor shrugged, reaching into his bag again. 'Well, what happened?'

'Palombo was waiting for me'—Cord stiffened for a moment as something wet and stinging swabbed his side—'waiting in the room in the dark.'

'Why?'

'He felt that way. I switched on the light, we started to talk, and someone cut loose with a machine-pistol from the gardens.'

'You saw where this man was?'

'Like hell. I was too busy getting clear.' Unpleasant things were being done along his ribs. He grunted a protest, and the doctor chuckled.

'M'sieu Cord, when a patient complains there is little wrong with him. The arm is a scratch. Your side'—he shrugged—'I would guess that was a ricochet. It glanced along a rib. Tomorrow it will feel like a well-kicked drum, but that is all. A little tape, a dressing, and I am finished.'

Rucos turned away, digging with a penknife around one of the bullet-holes in the plaster wall. He held out the result, a nine millimetre slug, standard machine-pistol ammunition. It meant little, but Cord's mouth tightened at the sight. The gunmen below had worked his first burst from right to left across the window. If it had been left to right it wouldn't be Palombo who would be on his way to emergency surgery.

The young Frenchman completed his task, made deprecating noises as Cord thanked him, then left. Rucos gestured the remaining gendarme to wait outside, then, as the door closed, his thin dark face hardened.

'You know why this happened, Mr Cord?'

'I can guess,' agreed Cord softly and bitterly.

'Your little story at the airport, that you would have information tonight—your "bait" Mr Cord. It was taken. But not when you expected.'

'All right,' snapped Cord, trapped by his own responsibility. 'But what about you, major? What about those men you said would be staked around?'

The grim beginnings of a smile came and died on Rucos's lips. 'They can report most of your actions during tonight. Most—not all. We Moroccans possess a certain delicacy in some matters. You understand?'

It was easiest not to answer.

Rucos shrugged. 'As for the gunman, that was my mistake, my responsibility. But I still ask myself whether what you said was bluff—or double-bluff.'

'And I'm beginning to wonder why you keep on asking,' grated Cord. He reached for his jacket with fingers which still hadn't quite steadied, found a cheroot, and lit it, as the door opened. A Moroccan in lieutenant's uniform looked in but stayed in the doorway. Rucos crossed over, they had a quick, low-voiced conversation, then the lieutenant departed.

Slowly, frowning, Rucos returned. 'You have a pistol.' It was more statement than question.

'Uh-huh.' Cord located his keys, and held them out. 'In my bag.'

Lips pursed, Rucos opened the bag, found the Neuhausen, and sniffed the barrel. Shaking his head, he carefully replaced the weapon and returned the keys.

'Well?' demanded Cord.

'Something strange.' The Moroccan used the swagger stick's tip to scratch the back of his neck, puzzled. 'We have found where the gunman waited, behind a bush. He wore European shoes'—he glanced at his own polished brogues—'which matters little. There were twenty fired cartridge cases, almost a full magazine. But there was also a large bloodstain, spreading over some of the cartridges. Other bloodstains, smaller, led from the bush to the outer wall.'

Cord whistled his surprise. 'It sounds like I'd a friend around. Any other trace of a struggle?'

'None. The only further report is of a car seen driving away, with no firm details.' The soldier didn't try to hide his bewilderment. '*Tiftikir* . . . the thing does not make sense.'

'Except that there were two men down in that garden, both watching, but with different reasons.' Cord chewed the cheroot thoughtfully. 'One had orders to kill if I made what looked like a contact. But the other—well, who'd want to give me a bodyguard?' The answer suddenly suggested itself. 'Sharif? Captain Sunner's in town. If he brought some of his men along . . .'

'We can find out,' said Rucos slowly. 'Sunner is here, waiting, wanting to see you.' He strode to the door, jerked it open, and beckoned along the corridor. 'Captain . . .'

Sunner strolled in, looked around the bullet-wrecked room with a casual professional interest, then gave an almost whimsical snicker.

'Thorough enough job. You were lucky, Cord.'

'Luckier than Palombo,' said Cord grimly.

'Perhaps for a reason.' Rucos addressed the mercenary with a slender hope in his voice. 'We believe someone tried to stop the gunman, probably wounded him. But this helper has disappeared. Now, if he was one of your men . . .'

'It wasn't.' Sunner was positive. 'The only passenger who came with me was Mathilde. My squad are too busy doing double guard up at the valley. And I was talking business with the Greeks when the shooting began.' He raised a cynical, questioning eyebrow. 'You haven't caught anyone?'

Rucos shook his head.

'Then what's to stop the same thing happening to-morrow, with President Sharif as target?'

'It will be daylight,' reminded Rucos, stiffening. 'We will take maximum precautions.'

'You'd damned well better,' growled Sunner. 'In case

you haven't heard, I've another V.I.P. from Jemma arriving in the morning. I can't afford any comic foul-ups —and if this is a sample of how a joint U.N.-Moroccan set-up comes unstuck, then I'm relying on my own measures.'

'Do that, Sunner, and you are *khalas* . . . finished.' Strain made Rucos lose control. 'Interfere, and I will have every one of your men disarmed and under guard. If President Sharif was not a guest of my nation it would have happened already.'

'Try it, you jumped-up peasant.' Sunner spat the words, his face twisted into a snarl of rage. 'Try it, and you'll land back in the mountains with no shoes on your feet.'

'And we have an excellent jail in Rabat, with no niceties about racial distinctions,' countered Rucos, starting forward.

'Ease up, both of you,' said Cord wearily, getting between them. 'Sunner, better get back to your Greeks. We've got troubles enough. And don't be a fool—if we start chopping and changing plans now, things will really land in the muck-heap.'

The antagonists glared at each other for another full minute. Then, abruptly, Sunner turned on his heel and marched out. The door slammed behind him.

Rucos drew a deep, quivering breath. 'Once, I would have killed that man.' Then, almost sheepishly, he shook his head. 'It would be awkward now.'

'Sunner rubs most people the wrong way,' said Cord with no particular sympathy. 'But Sharif is still his meal ticket. That gives him a right to be nervous.'

'And no one else?' Rucos grunted and glanced at his watch. 'I will leave two men downstairs, but nothing more should happen tonight. I will see some people, ask some questions, but . . .' his shrug was eloquent enough. 'Goodnight, Mr Cord. If there is positive news from the hospital I will make sure it reaches you.'

.　　　.　　　.　　　.　　　.

It was a minor luxury to be alone again. Gingerly, Cord eased himself into a fresh shirt then rested for a moment on the edge of the bed. Palombo's envelope—he brought it out, unfolded the sheet of coded groups it contained, and got to work.

Field Reconnaissance's standard code was a simple double-transposition affair. It took a few minutes of tight concentration to decipher the message from Andrew Beck, but the final result held its own surprises.

Rumoured Sharif offering swop Mahhabi sector Jemma territory for low-value Daman coastal strip as permanent peace solution. Daman likely accept deal. Arrival your area tomorrow, Abdul Zieull is anti-deal. Femma temperature now critical. Report.

Sharif the Peacemaker. It seemed far off character, even allowing for outside pressures. But Beck's signals had a habit of being hallmarked by solid fact. Whistling wryly between his teeth Cord lifted the telephone and asked for Maggie Delday's room.

She answered on the first ring, tension in her voice.

'Me,' he said soothingly. 'Everything all right?'

'Talos.' It came like a sigh. 'I tried to get to you, then tried to 'phone, but Major Rucos's men . . .'

'I can imagine.' He grinned a little. If he knew Rucos, it would be a long time before certain of his men forgot this night. 'Heard anything from Jackson?'

'Before the ambulance left. I saw him, and he said he'd

call if there was any news.' She hesitated. 'But you . . .'

'I'm still in one piece. I was luckier than Palombo. Now I need some help, Maggie. I've got to get a signal off— tonight, through your radio link. Will anyone be on duty if I go over?'

'Yes,' she said swiftly. 'There's a 24 hour watch. I'll come with you.'

'No. Stay where you are and wait for Jackson to call. Thanks, Maggie.'

Cord hung up before she could protest then reached for his jacket. Bloodstains apart, it was still in reasonable shape. He pulled it on, tucked the Neuhausen into the waistband of his slacks, and lifted the 'phone again.

The night manager was back at the hotel desk and immediately co-operative. Another room for m'sieu? One would be immediately ready, m'sieu's luggage would be transferred straight away.

Cord hung up, went out into the corridor, and saw one of Rucos's men lounging a few yards along. The gendarme stiffened.

'I'm changing rooms,' said Cord crisply. 'They're send-ing someone for my bag. You'll be around?'

The gendarme gave a stolid nod of agreement then backed it with a salute. Smiling his thanks, Cord headed for the elevator.

He found another gendarme prowling the hotel lobby and hung back behind a bank of potted palms, waiting for a diversion. It came as a cluster of customers made a noisy exit from the corner bar and he slipped past.

There were taxis waiting outside. He boarded the nearest and was on his way.

·   ·   ·   ·   ·

It took a long spell of doorbell ringing and knocking before a stooped, white-whiskered Arab night watchman let him into the UNESCO offices. Then came a brief argument, ended by a couple of silver dirhans, and at last he reached the radio room.

The operator was a tired-eyed, normally phlegmatic Irishman. He knew about Cord and he'd taken the incoming message from Beck. But now a 34 group code message with a priority prefix—the operator stared gloomily as Cord filled a full sheet of his signal pad.

'Ach well, it'll always pass the time,' he philosophised. 'Want an acknowledgement?'

'The reply will do,' said Cord. 'That should be in before morning.'

'More damned code?' The Irishman's gloom deepened as he reached for the switches. All this, and him with an unopened batch of local newspapers just arrived from home. Where was the justice in life?

Outside again, Cord heard locks click behind him as the watchman closed up. The street was empty, the night air crisp. He should have asked the taxi driver to wait—but there was no hurry about getting back.

Drooping over a high wall, an orange tree's laden branches hung low ahead. He plucked an orange, peeled it with a thumbnail, and sucked the juice schoolboy fashion as he began walking.

Nearly midnight Moroccan time. With a five-hour time difference that meant New York should receive the signal exactly when it would spoil Andrew Beck's evening meal. He grinned at the thought. Food was one of the bulky Field Reconnaissance chief's few conscious pleasures. But he'd get what was needed, and the answers might make things easier.

Strolling on, he passed a couple of Arabs sleeping in a doorway. One was an almost shapeless bundle, a blanket pulled over his head. A vegetable truck lumbered noisily down the road and swung off towards the Old Quarter. In the pale moonlight, the tall, black silhouette of the Affri suddenly showed ahead, lights still burning behind some of its windows.

The orange finished, he tossed it aside. Then, suddenly, he slowed as he rounded a curve in the road. A car was parked ahead, facing his way, an old, battered Citroen. There were no houses nearby, no gates in the high walls, no apparent reason for it being there. He saw the faint, momentary glow of a cigarette from the driver's side, then spotted another figure standing in the shadows beside the car.

Cord froze back into an equally dark patch of wall, his right hand touching the Neuhausen's butt. About a minute passed, then he heard hurrying footsteps. Someone was coming fast from the direction of the hotel.

The figure came into sight a moment later and passed under a streetlight. A tall woman wrapped in a native robe, her face was veiled.

An Arab woman on her own at that hour?

Cord eased the Neuhausen free and began to edge forward. The woman reached the car, stopped, and the front passenger door opened.

All he heard next was a soft rustle from behind. It might have been wind in the trees. But a lean, hard hand was suddenly over his mouth, the prick of sharp steel was at his throat.

'*Balaaf hival* . . . very still, friend.' The voice was low and harsh, all he could see of the man behind him was the dark, slim hand holding the knife. It had a plain bone handle and a short, straight blade honed to near enough a razor's edge. 'You understand?'

He nodded.

The man whistled twice, sharply. There was a single reply from the car.

'Now, friend. The gun in your hand—drop it. Then your face to the wall.'

Cord obeyed, the knife-point still pricking. The hand slipped from his mouth and was placed firmly over his eyes. It was rough and calloused and the owner was breathing with a quick excitement which held its own danger.

He heard the car start up, purr towards them, then stop. Doors clicked open, there were footsteps, then his captor spoke in a quick, tongue-clicking Arabic dialect. The hand was removed from his eyes, and next instant a coarse rag took its place and was firmly knotted blindfold style behind his head.

'Stay like that, Mr Cord,' said a different voice with an odd touch of amusement. 'Don't cook your blood pressure —we won't harm you if you behave. In fact, we've already saved you some trouble tonight.'

'At the hotel?' Cord turned his head a little. The knife-prick had gone, but he was pushed smartly in towards the wall again. 'Major Rucos is wondering what happened down in that garden.'

'If we'd been quicker, it wouldn't have happened at all. But we tried.'

He tried to analyse the man behind the words. Probably young, slightly sardonic, used to giving orders. The occasional soft blurring of a word meant an Arab, but one who spoke English with an easy, practised fluency.

'You wouldn't be El Aggahr?' he asked.

He heard a chuckle. Then a softer voice, a woman's

voice murmured for a moment.

'Maybe, maybe not,' said the man suddenly. 'Cord, you slightly embarrassed us a moment ago. But in a way this is useful. When you take Sharif round the power station tomorrow guard him carefully. Something very strange is shaping.'

'You should know,' shrugged Cord. 'I thought he was top of your hate list.'

'He is. But I want him in one piece—for the moment,' said the man behind him grimly.

'If you say so.' The woman must be close now. He could smell her perfume. It nudged a corner of his mind, nudged it without triggering the response it somehow should. 'What happens now?'

'Very little. Yacub has your gun and will stay until the car has gone. You will count to a hundred, slowly, then you can move. Understood?'

'I won't argue,' he agreed, waiting.

There were footsteps again, the car doors slammed and its engine started. As it drew away he began counting, reached twenty, then made a slow, experimental move of his hands towards the blindfold. Nothing happened. He drew a breath, ripped it off, and swung round.

The car was turning the corner, the street was empty, his gun was lying near his feet.

Swearing softly, Cord picked up the Neuhausen and caught a last glimpse of disappearing tail lights. Suddenly the perfume meant something.

Two minutes later he slipped back into the Affri's lobby. Rucos's man, a bored expression on his face, was sitting near the hotel desk reading a magazine in half-asleep style. Cord edged round a few paces, then approached the desk from the direction of the bar in confident fashion. Nodding to the gendarme, he picked up the house telephone and asked for Mathilde Dolanne's room.

There was no reply. He hadn't expected there would be. That clinging musk and roses perfume had only one user he knew about—which meant the strange, alarmingly beautiful girl had some unusual friends, friends he was certain Mohammed Sharif didn't know about.

He lifted the receiver again and this time asked for Maggie Delday. When she answered, her voice was sleepy.

'Any word yet, Maggie?'

'Yes. They think he'll live. Walt 'phoned just a little while back—he's staying at the hospital for now.' He heard a rustle and a click as she lit a cigarette, then she asked, 'Did you get the signal off?'

'Uh-huh.' He kept a cautious eye on the gendarme, but he looked sleepier than ever.

'Do you—well, want to come up?' She sounded suddenly shy, almost wary. 'For a drink or something?'

'No,' he assured her. 'I'm heading for bed. Good-night, Maggie.'

'G'night.' It came with something like relief, but half-stifled by a yawn.

His new room was on the top floor, and as he left the elevator the first thing he saw was Rucos's other man standing dourly by the door. The gendarme's face began to shape a scowl. He met it with a nod, a grin, and a pantomime of raising a glass to his lips. The man smiled.

There was no balcony in the new room. The bed had been moved as far as was humanly possible from the window.

The Affri didn't want any more incidents.

He felt the same way.

5

Talos Cord wakened around seven a.m. with daylight already pouring through the latticework of the window blinds. When he looked out, the roads below were busy with traffic. In the middle distance the tall minaret tower of the Koutoubia mosque, Marrakech's proudest landmark, was sun-tinted a deep pink amid its nest of palms and cedars. The morning, at least, seemed set for fair.

He checked the corridor and found the police guard had gone. A call to room service brought a coffee and rolls breakfast. Cord shaved, then ate while he dressed. Walter Jackson arrived as he was coughing through his first cigarette.

' 'Morning.' Tired-eyed, unusually pale, the Australian limped over to a chair and sank down. 'Well, how do you feel now?'

'Reasonable.' It wasn't quite accurate. The arm was almost its usual self but his side felt as if he'd been stood on by a camel—a heavily built camel. 'What about Palombo?'

'Coming on.' Jackson grimaced a little. He was unshaven and his shirt was crumpled. 'I spent the night at the hospital. They got the bullets out and he's sleeping now. Maggie's gone over.'

'It was a rough deal for him.'

'Meaning they were really gunning for you?' Jackson nodded. 'That's how I reckoned it.'

Cord didn't enlighten him. That could keep for a later time. 'Seen Major Rucos?'

'Just before I came here. He's running around in ever-

89

decreasing circles.' A glint of humour entered the weary voice. 'That character's going to end up like the original ooja bird, disappearing in a puff of smoke. He said to tell you this 'plane with Abdul what's-his-name aboard should arrive around 8.15. Want us to be there?'

'We'd better, just to show interest,' decided Cord. 'Any word of a radio message for me?'

'Over our set? I haven't looked in at the office so far.' Yawning, Jackson gestured towards the bathroom. 'Mind if I freshen up a little, save myself a hike?'

'Go ahead. There's a razor on the shelf.' Cord finished his cigarette then had another while the man ran water and splashed around. When Jackson emerged again he looked nearer his usual self.

'Ready?' queried Cord.

'For most things,' agreed Jackson soberly. 'I was thinking. I've one advantage in all this. One look at me'—he slapped his heavy paunch—'well, nobody's going to mistake who they're aiming at.' A rumbling chuckle took the edge from the words. 'Let's go then. I've got Roder and the station wagon outside.'

They left the hotel. Parked at the kerb, the engine pulsing a cloud of white exhaust, the station wagon's roof and windows still bore a liberal coating of overnight condensation. Behind the wheel, Roder Hassabou wore a sheepskin waistcoat over his usual sweater and slacks.

'*Sahlan,* Mr Cord,' he greeted sympathetically. 'You feel okay now?'

'More or less.' As the doors closed and they started off he eyed the Arab thoughtfully. 'Where were you when all the excitement was on?'

'Me?' Roder gave an almost regretful shrug. 'At the *sinima,* Mr Cord. A Western.'

'Cowboys and Indians.' Jackson rumbled his disgust. 'I've seen some—British actors, American money, shot in Spain by an Italian crew then dubbed in Arabic. Well, was it any good?'

'Much shooting, Mr Jackson.' A cherubic smile creased the thin, high-cheeked features. 'Very good.'

Set on the fringe of town. the airport had a heavy sprinkling of armed police guarding its entrance and the approach to the terminal building. The station wagon's U.N. badges took them through, a sergeant guided them onto the runway apron, then they got out, left Roder, and walked across to the assembled welcoming party.

Stiffly erect in uniform, Captain Sunner waited beside a large chauffeur-driven Mercedes. A few paces away, studiously ignoring him, Major Rucos glanced at his watch as he talked to a trio of airport officials. In the background a huddle of khaki-uniformed Moroccan army men clustered around their escort vehicles.

Sunner was nearest and seemed pleased to see them.

'On your own?' Disappointed, Cord raised a questioning eyebrow. 'Where's Mathilde—I thought she'd be along.'

'The Greeks needed someone to nursemaid them for a spell this morning.' Sunner showed a trace of displeasure. 'They're going off sight-seeing—President Sharif doesn't want to meet them until tomorrow.'

'When he'll sign the contracts?'

'Probably.' The man frowned at the sky, then brightened. 'This looks like the 'plane now.'

It was. As the dot on the north-east sky shaped into a slim twin-jet executive aircraft, Cord eased towards Rucos.

'On schedule, major?'

'Their aircraft, their schedule,' said Rucos shortly. 'I hear there is good news about your director, Palombo. You must be glad.'

Cord nodded wryly at the underlying inference. 'Any developments?'

Rucos pursed his lips, watching the 'plane lower its wheels and begin a final approach. 'So far, no. But that does not mean we have stopped trying. And if you come across any information which might help . . .'

'Tell you,' Cord finished for him, nodding.

But he qualified it to himself. Andrew Beck had said it first, with his usual irritating habit of being right. Don't take anyone or anything at face value. He would have to be sure who would benefit before he relied or confided too much anywhere.

Touchdown smooth, the aircraft taxied on on a dying whine of jets and stopped within a few yards of the reception party. Hydraulics pulsed, a door opened, and a flight of steps folded down. First out was a uniformed crewman, then Sunner went striding forward as the next figure appeared in the doorway.

Abdul Zieull, an elderly, ascetic figure wearing a burnouse over a lightweight fawn business suit, came down slowly. He acknowledged Sunner's salute with little more than a nod but seemed very pleased to have solid ground under his feet again. Rucos came forward, was introduced, and the three men talked for a minute or so. Then the newly arrived politician began walking towards Cord and Jackson.

Once again Sunner made the introductions. Jackson was first, then Cord's turn came. He was raked by a pair of sunken, bird-like eyes and received a brief, bony-fingered handshake.

'United Nations.' A faint smile touched the Arab's mouth. 'You are the people who would stop us cutting too many Daman throats.'

'There's nothing personal in it,' said Cord placidly. 'We're just against throat-cutting in general.'

'But with no real power to stop it.' A thin finger wagged in positive emphasis. 'That is your weakness. Big wars you can stop—because neither side wants them. But a little war? You are helpless.' He chuckled, savouring the word, and turned away.

'Old devil,' muttered Jackson under his breath. 'Don't they have any other kind in Jemma?'

'I'm beginning to wonder,' admitted Cord.

Followed by Sunner, the politician boarded the Mercedes. As the doors closed and it glided off the Moroccan escort detail sprang to life. Exhausts roaring, a trio of motor cyclists took the lead. Immediately behind them came an army scout car, twin .5 machine guns cocked and ready. At the rear of the Mercedes another scout car slotted in, then two more motor-cycle outriders.

'Ready to take on a flaming army,' grunted Jackson, trying to appear unimpressed. 'Well, that's another little job done—but where the blazes is Roder?'

Cord looked around. Major Rucos was talking to the aircraft's pilot, a red-headed European. A refuelling truck was backing into position. But their driver had vanished. Swearing impatiently, Jackson leaned into the station wagon and placed his hand flat on the horn ring. At the second blast, Roder ambled into sight from the direction of the terminal building, an innocently surprised expression on his face.

'Time to go, Mr Jackson?'

'Hell, no—I do this for fun.' Jackson lowered himself

into the front seat and hauled his leg aboard. 'Come on, Cord.'

'In a minute.' Cord left them, went towards the 'plane, and got Rucos to one side.

'That was one very organised escort you laid on. Same this afternoon?'

'Bigger.' Rucos warmed to the compliment. 'You found Zieull interesting?'

'Interesting—and probably as hard as nails.'

Rucos nodded agreement. 'You will be surprised at what he told me. He will be at the power station—he flies back to Jemma afterwards. But he is here to have a row with Sharif. To "sort him out" is how I think you would put it.'

'Did he say why?'

'I did not ask. It was not my place.'

The station wagon's horn blew again. Cord grinned. 'We'll be at the site before twelve. You'll be there?'

'Then or soon afterwards,' said Rucos soberly. 'For once I may be a good Muslim and say my noon prayer. If there is any real help above, I want it on my side today.'

.   .   .   .   .

Le Sud hospital was big, new, and had an atmosphere mainly compounded of antiseptic and floor polish. Walt Jackson led Cord through a maze of corridors to the start of a private ward and spoke to a Moroccan orderly at the inquiry desk. The orderly asked them to wait and went off. In a couple of minutes a plump, middle-aged French nursing sister came towards them, Maggie Delday at her side.

'M'sieu Jackson.' The sister smiled a greeting. 'Your friend Palombo is a most tenacious young man. He is doing well.'

'Can we see him?' asked Cord.

'He's asleep, Talos,' said Maggie. Back in shirt and slacks again, her face bare of make-up, she showed less confidence than the older woman. 'They've got him sedated to the eyebrows.' She shrugged a little. 'He woke up for a moment a while back, and managed to say hello —that was all.'

'Which is as it should be,' said the sister firmly. 'But you can look, m'sieu.'

Cord went with her to a sideroom door. She opened it quietly. Palombo's bed was against one wall of the cubicle. Lying under the sheets, the UNESCO man had his eyes closed. A blood drip tube ran from a stand to somewhere on his left arm. Against the white pillow, his pale face seemed younger than ever without spectacles.

Peering over Cord's shoulder, Jackson grunted. 'How long till we can talk to him, sister?'

She frowned. 'Certainly not today, m'sieu. He improves, but his condition is still serious. But if you leave a message, I will keep it with the others.'

'You've some already?' queried Cord.

'Some!' Her hands formed a silent exclamation. They drew back and she closed the door. 'There is even one from the Imperial Palace, another from this President Sharif, and many from friends.'

Jackson grinned. 'Then you'd better give him the V.I.P. treatment to match. Just tell him we've been around, sister.' He turned to Maggie Delday. 'Doesn't seem much sense in anyone staying for now. Coming?'

She nodded, thanked the sister, and they left.

Outside the building, Maggie took a deep breath then let it go in a slow sigh.

'Tired?' queried Cord.

Their eyes met and he saw something there which might have been a faint hostility. She shook her head almost curtly.

'I just don't like hospitals.'

'There are worse places, once you get to know your way around.' Jackson yawned and flexed his shoulders. 'Anyway, we'd better get some work done. Want to come along, Cord? You could check whether that signal's arrived. Then, if you give me another hour or so, I'll collect you from the Affri and we'll head for the nuclear site. Right?'

'Suits me,' he agreed. 'What about you, Maggie? Not coming for the grand inspection?'

'No,' she said flatly. 'I've too much else to do.'

.   .   .   .   .

Roder drove them over to the UNESCO building and dropped them at the front door. Once inside, Jackson grunted a farewell and headed off.

'Maggie . . .' Cord laid a hand on her arm. 'Mad at me?'

'Not at you—myself.' She turned away from him for a moment, looking around the empty hallway. 'No, that's not right either. Just—well, this time yesterday everything was neat and orderly. Now there's Joe Palombo lucky to be alive, anything liable to happen next, and you.'

'I won't be around for long,' he said quietly. 'You know that.'

'Maybe that's another part of what's wrong.' She forced a smile. 'Anyway, I'll see you when you get back from Safi.'

'Count on it.' He paused for a moment, still holding her arm. 'Maggie, will you do a couple of things for me, no questions asked?'

She frowned, but nodded.

'I want a check on the personnel files. First thing, to find out the exact date Roder went on the payroll and which oil company he claimed he'd been with before. Second, a check if anyone on staff—anyone from Joe Palombo down—has ever been stationed in Jemma or Rahad. Can you do that?'

'Fairly easily.' She bit her lip, far from happy. 'I won't like doing it. But if it matters...'

'It does. And thanks.' He kissed her quickly but firmly on the lips. 'Call that a downpayment.'

The radio room came next. When Cord got there the duty operator, a burly, gum-chewing Canadian, grinned at his query.

'It's here all right. Came in just before I took over duty —and believe me, you weren't popular.'

Cord thanked him, took the coded slip, and settled in an empty chair by the window. Translated, Andrew Beck's growl lurked behind every word of the curt cablese.

No report geo-surveys in Jemma or Daman. Alleged archaeological investigation Jemma last year, Greek sponsored, was in area you suggest. Up-follow quickliest. Query two, George Sunner ex-British Colonial Army dismissed service after allegations brutality. Ends.

Carefully, conscious of the operator's silent curiosity, he touched the cheroot's lighted end to the paper, let it smoulder for a moment, then dropped it into an ashtray.

'Like that?' queried the operator as the message continued to burn.

'It could be. Any other copies?'

There were none. He waited until the last of the paper had charred from sight, thanked the man, and left.

Outside, the day was warming . . . in more ways than one, mused Cord. He began walking back towards the Affri, moving slowly along the crowded street, ignoring the small boys selling chewing gum, single cigarettes and more surprising items.

The information on Sunner was no more than he'd expected. But the rest—that really mattered.

That there had been no official geo-survey didn't surprise him. The combine the Greeks represented had gained their knowledge, obviously with Jemma government co-operation, in a way that made big business sense. In any game where the stakes were potentially big it didn't pay to shout your intentions.

It was where they'd operated that held the punch. Some inner devil had prompted Cord to query the northern coastal strip. And the inner devil had been right.

The Greeks were ready to sign a deal—while Mohammed Sharif was apparently busy making wily, conciliatory noises to his irate next-door neighbours. If Field Reconnaissance's information was right, if Sharif put through the deal of swapping his Mahhabi minority sector for part of Daman's coastal territory, a deal which on the face of things favoured Daman all the way . . .

The rest was as smooth as a confidence trick. Sharif got rid of the Mahhabi thorn in his side and gained—gained just what apart from two coastal sectors side by side?

And the tension, the violence, the threat of near-war which brought the whole possibility into being? Was it too fantastic to believe it was all part of the same elaborate, high-stakes game?

Cord could think of only one way to edge nearer the truth. When he reached the Affri he ambled casually towards the lobby desk.

'Is Mr Pauol in—I can't remember his room number.'

'A moment, m'sieu.' The desk clerk glanced briefly at the register then the keyboard. 'No, m'sieu. He is in 342, but all the Greek gentlemen have gone out for the day. We expect them back this evening.'

'It can wait.' Cord nodded his thanks and strolled towards the elevator.

First stop was his own room, to collect a little Swedish penknife from his travel bag. It had a multiplicity of blades and sold commercially as a sportsman's companion. But that was incidental, and one or two of the blades were slightly altered from the original. A couple of experimental probings at his own doorlock and he decided on a narrow blade with a curved spur ending.

He used the staircase down to Pauol's floor, checked the corridor was empty, then crossed over to the room door. Ten seconds with the picklock and it clicked open. He slipped inside and closed the door gently behind him.

Apparently the Greek had a good expense account. He was in a large, well-furnished lounge, with a half-opened bedroom door leading off. Cord took another step forward then froze. Someone was in there, moving quietly. He heard a sigh, then renewed activity.

On tip-toe, he moved nearer, saw further into the bedroom, then grinned. Mathilde Dolanne was standing beside the bed, frowning down at an opened suitcase, rummaging through its contents with a tight-lipped concentration. Still on tip-toe, he reached the doorway and stopped.

'Lost something, Mathilde?' he asked cheerfully.

The slim figure, incongruously neat in a blue linen dress, jerked as if she'd been slapped hard across the face.

99

She turned slowly, her face paling beneath the bronze-like tan.

'You.' She drew a breath, keeping surprising control. 'Why are you here?'

'That was going to be my question,' countered Cord blandly. He saw her eyes flicker towards the matching blue leather handbag on the bed, moved quickly, and got it before she did. 'Mind?'

She shrugged, her face expressionless as he opened the bag. Inside, stowed separate from the rest of the contents, was a tiny bone-handled .22 Beretta.

'Nice,' he said conversationally, balancing it in his hand. 'Every girl should have one.'

'Perhaps with reason.' Eyes angry, she watched as he laid down the bag but slipped the gun in his pocket. 'What do you want?'

'Probably the same as you.' He nodded towards the suitcase. 'Unless you make a habit of this.'

'I'—her hands tightened by her sides—'I am preparing a minute of last night's meeting. Captain Sunner must deliver it to the president later today, and there is a point I wanted to check. As they are all out, I . . .'

'Got through a locked door and did some private research,' finished Cord with a dry sarcasm. 'That's what I call devotion to duty. What's more, you say it like you meant it.' He came over, grinned as she edged back, and glanced at the papers she'd already spread beside the suitcase. 'You get around, Mathilde. But maybe a little too much, like last night. The Arab robes were fine but the perfume—no, that gave it away.'

'I don't understand.' She turned away, fixing her attention on a reproduction painting on the opposite wall. It was an uninspired futuristic affair, mostly blood-red cubes. 'I heard about the shooting, of course—and what happened to Palombo. It was regrettable.'

'That they hit Palombo—or that they missed me?' Cord considered her thoughtfully for a moment then shook his head. 'No, I don't think you were in on that act, Mathilde. Not after meeting your little friend with the knife. Otherwise my throat wouldn't still be in one piece.'

She didn't answer and he turned back to the papers. The European combine was named as Interlak Exploration—which meant nothing and certainly rated as nothing more than a dummy holding company. The first few sheets were technical reports. Their subject made him whistle.

'Rutile'—the term for that high-grade mineral sand clicked against a memory of distant high school science—'titanium dioxide? That's what it's about?'

'These are private papers,' she reminded tartly.

'I'm the kind who likes reading other people's mail,' he said absently, keeping on. Survey ratings, work schedules, labour to production costs—unrefined rutile sand looked like gritty grey-black caviar. But when it was found in workable quantities, when it was processed and became titanium dioxide, it meant a bonanza.

As a chemical it was vital in a dozen different industries. Fully refined, as titanium, it was a light, tough temperature-resistant metal vital in supersonic flight, missiles and space capsules.

Jemma might have no oil. But she'd found something offering equal riches. If the strike extended north, beyond her boundaries into Daman, several pieces of the puzzle fell into place.

He searched for a map. The only one was a small,

photo-copied sheet, circled at a point on the coast well south of the border.

'What's this?' he demanded.

'You should know,' she retorted. 'That's where the aid programme power station would be built. Interlak would have their processing plant next door.'

'And the area they'd be working?'

She shrugged evasively. 'The president says the agreement is for the general rights. Exact locations would come later.'

'You're sure?' Cord saw the grey-green eyes flicker and smiled a little. 'No, you're not, Mathilde. My guess is that's why you're here—whoever you're working for.'

'I told you . . .'

'Don't,' he said, almost wearily. 'I'm going to take a look around.'

It took about five minutes to check the bedroom and the main apartment, and he drew a blank. When he returned, the girl had the suitcase re-packed and was closing the lid.

'Was it locked?'

She hesitated then nodded. Silently, she put a hand deep inside the neck of her dress, wriggled a little, and brought out a key. He took it from her. The metal was roughly shaped, still warm and moist from her body. The locks clicked shut and she put the suitcase back on a chair before carefully smoothing the rumpled bedcover.

'Come on.' He took her firmly by the arm, guided her out into the lounge and pushed her towards a chair. 'How'd you fix the key?'

'It'—she gnawed her lip—'it was arranged.'

'You're organised,' he admitted. 'Sit down. We're going to talk.'

She obeyed.

'All right, Mathilde. What's the story?'

'You mean Maggie Delday hasn't told you?' she queried tartly. Then, suddenly, she chuckled and stretched back in cat-like fashion. 'But is Maggie Delday such a saint? Suppose you tell me that.'

He shrugged. 'You're walking a tightrope, Mathilde. If Sharif found you double-crossing him he'd play rough, maybe even turn you over to Sunner. A nasty little customer, Captain Sunner.'

'I have seen him question people.' The words came flatly, with a cold bitterness. Then she shook her head. 'But you will not tell them, Talos Cord. You still don't know who to trust, whose side you are really on.' She rose and came towards him, smiling strangely. 'You looked very unhappy with that knife at your neck. Just here . . .' one long, cool finger touched the spot. 'And I will tell you one thing about Mohammed Sharif. He is older than he looks. He'—her eyes crinkled—'he is no longer capable of enjoying some things, though he keeps a reminder of them beside him.'

'Only a reminder?'

'For most practical purposes? Yes.' She was very close now. When she half-turned, her breast brushed against him. 'Should we go now?'

'After you,' said Cord politely. Andrew Beck wouldn't have believed it. But Beck didn't have an ache in his side which was beginning to throb like an overworked drum.

He remembered the Beretta and brought it out. 'You'd better have this back.'

She stowed it in her handbag, then they left the room together and took the elevator down to the hotel foyer. As they got out, she glanced towards the corner bar.

'You could buy me a drink.'

'I could, but not now,' answered Cord. 'When do you see Sharif next?'

'I go back to Mihmaaz this evening.'

'And the Greeks arrive there tomorrow?'

She nodded.

'Mathilde'—Cord brought her round towards him—'just what is your angle?'

'Partly keeping Sharif alive, for now anyway,' she said steadily. 'The rest doesn't matter to you. Except . . .'

'Well?'

Her mouth tightened again. 'Talos, something I don't understand is happening. We—the people I am helping expected a certain situation but there is something else. We are puzzled, uneasy.'

'You've got company on that,' he said heavily.

'It hardly helps.' Mathilde gave a faint, oddly wry smile. 'Maybe there'll be a chance to tell you more some day. If you wanted, that is. We—well, we wouldn't have to talk all the time.' The smile became slightly softer at the edges. 'I'd like that, I think.'

She had turned and was gone before he could answer.

.　　　.　　　.　　　.　　　.

Walt Jackson arrived exactly on schedule. Outside the hotel, Roder waited with the station wagon's engine ticking over. The moment they were aboard he set it moving.

The warm, dusty journey west to Safi went smoothly but with an undercurrent of tension. Most of the way Jackson talked loud and fast, his humour forced. Even Roder seemed affected, speaking only when he had to and then in short, monosyllabic fashion.

The kilometre stones slipped past in monotonous procession, then, close on noon, they were skirting the out-skirts of Safi and could see the blue of the Atlantic. Near Cap Cantin, a dark blue bus filled with armed gendarmes was unloading a detail of men at a bridge—and when the half-finished bulk of the Enveena generating station appeared ahead the main gate looked more like the entrance to an army post.

Carbine-carrying sentries waved them through into a parking area already occupied by a selection of army trucks, jeeps and a field kitchen unit. As the station wagon stopped, Major Rucos jumped down from a camouflage painted command truck and came towards them, glancing at his watch.

'*Aywa* . . . good, you are on time,' he greeted as they climbed out. 'And we have just had word from Sharif's convoy. They have left the valley.'

Jackson grunted and looked around. 'Where's Tom Fielden?'

'Here.' The bushy-haired site agent answered for himself, pushing angrily through a cluster of guards. 'Walt, just who the hell is running things inside this fence—us or the Moroccans?'

'It's what's called an exercise in mutual co-operation,' said Cord dryly. 'Correct, major?'

'As we agreed,' murmured Rucos.

'It hasn't looked that way,' growled Fielden, subsiding a little. 'Well, we did what you wanted, Cord—all-night perimeter guards, the lot. We had a couple of false alarms, but nothing really happened.'

'*Lissa* . . . so far it is peaceful,' agreed the Moroccan soberly. 'That almost worries me in itself.'

They spent the next half-hour in a detailed inspection tour of the Enveena site, from the camp drawing office transformed into a reception room all the way down to the shore-level pump-house blocks. Jackson limped along stubbornly with the rest, but his exhaustion was plain by the time they'd finished.

An ice-cold beer from the camp stock helped him recover. Some of Rucos's men brought them plates of couscous cooked army style—a hot, peppery dish of wheat grains and vegetables with all the subtle palate impact of an explosion.

The waiting time passed slowly, punctuated by the occasional radio message from the approaching convoy. Then, just after two p.m., it appeared.

First came a helicopter, blades chunking less than a hundred feet above the roadway as it scouted the route. Then a lone motor cyclist, red light flashing, roared up to the camp gate and braked in a way which brought his rear wheel skidding round.

The main party arrived moments later in fractionally more sedate style. Framed in a positive pack of motor cyclists, heavily armed scout cars fore and aft, President Sharif's big, blue bullet-proof Rolls-Royce purred in with his personal standard flying up front. Captain Sunner was beside the driver. At the rear, looking fairly pleased with life, Mohammed Sharif was arrayed in full tribal robes and had Abdul Zieull seated on his left.

Immediately behind them came the Mercedes, carrying half-a-dozen of Sunner's blue-uniformed mercenaries. They were tough, tanned scowling men who knew their jobs. Almost before the convoy had stopped they were out, machine-pistols discreetly ready.

The formal welcoming session got under way. Cord hung back from it, watching the helicopter land in a flurry of dust at the far end of the parking lot. Roder was over there, an interested spectator.

'Cord . . .'

He turned, and saw Jackson beckoning him over.

'We're ready to start the tour,' said the Australian in a slightly perturbed voice. He glanced at Sharif, who seemed amused about something. 'However it happens His Excellency would prefer to confine himself to seeing the basic layout and studying the project model.'

'After my illness, the entire tour might be rather strenuous,' murmured Mohammed Sharif. A small, gold-ringed hand waved at Abdul Zieull, whose face was as expressionless as a roll of leather. 'My Minister of Internal Affairs is well qualified to inspect the project in depth. So I will leave that to him—while you and I, Mr Cord, occupy ourselves less arduously.'

'If that's what you want,' said Cord easily. 'But I'm no expert. Perhaps if Jackson . . .'

'I want you, Mr. Cord.' The black beard stiffened along Sharif's jawline, his lips shaped something close to a pout of irritation. 'Agreed?'

Nobody argued. Smiling a little, Sharif waved them on their way. Only Sunner looked like hanging back, until Sharif flicked his hand in a curt dismissal.

The main party set off, down the path towards the shore. Suddenly, Cord heard the Arab chuckle.

'*Tamalli* . . . always delegate when you can,' declared Sharif briskly. He glanced over his shoulder. Sunner's tall, thin sergeant was waiting patiently in the background. So were two of the Moroccans. 'Where are the rest of my men?'

'Getting something to eat,' Cord told him. 'We arranged things that way—Sunner was happy enough about it.'

'If he is ever really happy about anything I would be surprised.' Sharif gave a small shrug beneath the flowing robes. 'At least he is efficient. Now, show me this model.'

The three-man escort tailed them to the door of the office hut, where Sharif gestured them to wait. Inside, Cord led the way to the back room where Tiny Town was displayed.

'Ah.' Sharif purred his interest. 'This, at least, I can understand. Which is the generating station?'

'This section.' Cord showed him, trying to remember some of the facts he'd been fed earlier. 'It'll be an advanced gas-cooled reactor, producing around 400 megawatts.'

Sharif nodded, scratching his stomach through the heavy robes. '*Ya salaam* . . . these itch. Allah alone knows how my fathers survived in such clothes. If this was not an official occasion—but never mind. Where is the water-making plant?'

'The long block next door. It's a multi-stage unit.'

'And it will produce much?'

'Around seventy million gallons of drinking water a day, distilled sea water.'

'For Jemma, even half as much would be a miracle.' Sharif stared at the model, gnawing lightly on a tendril of beard. 'And the cost?'

'For this, around a hundred million dollars—part interest-free loan, the rest in direct aid.'

'The same terms have been offered to us, though the cost would be less, for a smaller unit.' Sharif abandoned the model. 'But now with conditions. You know about them?'

'I'd heard,' said Cord carefully.

'Terms—or blackmail.' The Arab's small nostrils

flared. 'First, your people say, there must be a guarantee of peace. They say this to me—not to Daman, not to the Mahhabi vermin there or their kin in Jemma.'

'Daman has had its own warnings,' murmured Cord.

Sharif ignored him, scowling. 'Assassination, raiding, killing—your man Palombo, my brother-in-law Wat Said. It is all the same to scum like this renegade El Aggahr. Make no mistake, Cord, we are close to the brink. Abdul Zieull comes here panting for war as the answer—and it would be a war we could win in a week.'

'Stage one only,' said Cord pointedly. 'It wouldn't stop there.'

'No.' Sharif gave a humourless smile. 'I would be a fool to believe that. So I have another answer—which was the other reason why Zieull came here. He is a stubborn old fool, but I needed his support. It took time, and he is still unhappy. But if our Mahhabi want to belong to Daman then we will let them.'

'Just like that?' Cord feigned surprise.

'An exchange of territory. We would want a small, use-less sector of Daman in exchange—useless, but necessary for the balance of pride. The hint has been made already, and Daman is interested. That way I get rid of the Mahhabi problem and keep your U.N. aid. Perhaps'— Sharif eyed him craftily—'perhaps even gain more, as a gesture of gratitude.'

'I'd call that blackmail in reverse.' Cord grinned openly. This fat, bearded politician was playing his hand with a craftsman's cunning. He decided to try a little of the same game. 'How does the Greek syndicate fit in the picture? They mumbled about mineral rights when I met them.'

'They have hopes, and we will grant them concessions.' Warily, Sharif sidestepped the rest. 'Obviously any foreign investor looks for a settled, peaceful climate.'

'Plus power and water if they decide to start mining?'

'If . . . when . . .' Sharif shrugged his apparent disinterest. 'Such possibilities are long-term. Any possibility which helps Jemma develop should be encouraged.'

Cord thought of the figures on the survey schedules, the current price per ton of high-grade rutile ore, but said nothing.

'I should see a little of what is outside now,' said Sharif suddenly. 'But remember, Mr Cord. You can advise your Secretariat that I am at least trying for this peace—advise them, and perhaps indicate they should show gratitude if peace is accomplished.'

They went back out into the hot, still air where Sergeant Denke and the two Moroccans were still patiently waiting. Making no attempt to hide his boredom, Sharif allowed himself to be guided through the nearer sections of construction work. He said little and only brightened when the main party suddenly appeared some distance away, coming along a gravelled path towards them.

'The tour is over?'

'Almost,' nodded Cord. 'That's the reactor tower base they're leaving. All that's left is . . .'

He didn't get finishing. The pathway ahead disappeared in a sudden roaring flash. As the blast echoed and died, debris pattered down—and Abdul Zieull's party had disappeared in a curtain of dust and smoke.

For a moment, not another sound broke the air. All around, guards and staff stared open-mouthed at that lingering curtain of grey-red dust. Then, suddenly, came reaction. People began running. Denke and the two Moroccans swept close around President Sharif like a human shield.

'Stay there.' Cord shouted the words over his shoulder and went sprinting down the path. When he reached the spot, the dust was still settling. A deep crater had been blasted in the centre of the pathway. To one side a Moroccan soldier lay twisted, bloody and dead. Another was near, on his knees, groaning, clutching his middle.

Skirting the crater, he passed them then stopped with a sigh of relief. Abdul Zieull was being helped to his feet, apparently intact. Nearby, also trying to rise again but having trouble with his artificial leg, Walt Jackson was swearing like a trooper.

'Cord'—Major Rucos floundered towards him, blood from a small gash on his forehead streaking down through the dust which coated his dark face—'where's the president?'

'Back there, in one piece. What about here?'

The Moroccan shook his head in open agitation. 'I had two men on ahead. It caught them. No one else is hurt. We were too far back.'

'Luck,' said Cord grimly.

'Luck?' Rucos stared past him at the dead man, at the other Moroccan now being tended by a cluster of helpers. 'Perhaps—but how did it happen? This place was guarded, we had it checked . . .' he broke off and began barking orders for a stretcher party.

Abdul Zieull stalked past them, a tall, angry figure. Captain Sunner kept close in his wake, giving a glare as he went past.

.　　　.　　　.　　　.　　　.

The initial shock over, Rucos took firm control again. Loaded into a car, the wounded man was despatched to Safi with a siren-screaming motor cycle escort in attendance. Jackson had to be half-helped, half-carried back, still cursing, demanding to know where Roder had got to, explaining that something had smashed the knee-joint of his artificial leg.

Sharif and Abdul Zieull were in the main office block, a tight ring of guards outside, their cars already being brought round. After a few minutes, Sunner left the hut and marched pale-faced along the pathway to where Cord and Rucos were hunkered down beside the crater.

'I warned you,' he snarled as he reached them. 'I warned you, but you wouldn't listen.'

Wearily, Rucos looked up. 'It was my men who were in front, Sunner. Where were you?'

'Not far behind you.' Sunner swallowed hard. 'What difference does it make?'

Rucos shrugged. 'Very little. At least we know what happened—or Cord does.'

'Radio-controlled anti-personnel mine,' said Cord grimly, nodding at the scatter of metallic fragments they'd managed to gather. 'It fired on a signal—which could have come from well outside the fence. The fellow on the other end was just too eager when he pressed that button, otherwise he'd have hit the jackpot.'

'From outside or inside,' snapped Sunner. 'It could be one of your people, Cord. What about that damned driver you tote around? Jackson can't find him.'

'Roder?' Cord glanced sharply, questioningly at Rucos.

'No.' Rucos was positive. 'I had that thought, among others. He has the best of alibis, Sunner. He was talking to your own driver when it happened.'

'But we can guess how it got there,' said Cord softly. 'One of those "false alarms" last night was for real. Someone got in, probably through the seaward side, and planted the mine—this path had to be used if any tour was under way. After that, they just watched and waited.'

'Well, President Sharif isn't waiting,' said Sunner icily. 'We're leaving now. And I'm changing the return route—I'm taking no more chances.' He swung away from the Moroccan. 'Cord, he wants to see you first. I'd advise you to come.'

Cord sighed, rose to his feet, and went with him.

With its untouched tables of food and drink the reception room looked the setting for a wake which had gone wrong.

Jackson sat to one side, a cigarette jammed in his mouth, the damaged leg stretched useless in front of him. In the middle of the floor, the two Arab politicians listened stony-faced while a nervously confused Fielden made apologetic noises.

'Enough.' Sharif waved him aside as Cord entered. Thick lips twisted in a scowl, his small eyes bright with anger, the president was in no mood for small-talk. 'Well, Cord—what can you tell us?'

'Very little yet, apart from what caused it,' said Cord, knowing a different kind of explosion was due. 'We're doing all we can.'

'The same as in New York?' queried Zieull from the rear, contempt in the words. 'When such things happen the cause is incompetence—or worse.'

A low growl of agreement came from deep in Sharif's throat. 'Cord, I gave you one message—and now this is another for your U.N. preachers of peace. I will still make this last try—my offer to Daman will stand. But not for long. In three days I fly home. When I arrive, either

Daman must have agreed to what I have proposed or we attack. You understand?'

.   .   .   .   .

Five minutes later the Rolls-Royce and its escorts swept out of camp. Propped against the hut doorway, leaning perilously on his stick, Walt Jackson shook a sad head.

'There goes trouble,' he said laconically. 'Trouble any way you look at it.' He stopped, his red face registering almost comical surprise. 'Well, look who's decided to honour us now.'

Grinning self-consciously, Roder Hassabou strolled towards them. 'You want me, Mr Jackson?'

'You know damned well I do,' declared Jackson in a yelp of relieved fury. 'Where the devil did you disappear to this time?'

Roder grimaced apologetically. 'I was helping people.'

'Well, now you can damned well help me back to that station wagon,' answered Jackson.

'You're going?' Tom Fielden frowned unhappily. 'You too, Cord?'

Cord nodded.

'What's to stay for?' grunted Jackson.

'Nothing. Fielden scratched his head. 'Except I've eight hundred dirhan's worth of catering in that reception room. What do I do with it?'

Jackson told him, in fine detail.

6

The light was dulling down to dusk as the station wagon made its way in through the beginnings of Marrakech's evening rush-hour. They stopped at the Affri, off-loaded Walt Jackson, and he made a cursing, hopping progression into the hotel lobby supported by two porters, a third coming behind carrying the shattered leg with uneasy, awkward care.

Once Jackson had gone, Cord sank into the front passenger seat and told Roder to take him to the project offices.

Yawning a little, the Arab nodded and set the station wagon moving. The traffic was thickening, heavy with pedal cycles and motor scooters, the riders dressed in everything from hooded robes to sweat shirts and jeans.

'Any more gossip from the *suk*?' asked Cord suddenly.

'No, Mr Cord.' Roder shook his head. 'But *laazim aruuh* . . . I must go to see friends tonight. Maybe I ask them, eh?' His slim hands twirled the wheel, they avoided killing a cyclist, and took a corner seconds before the gendarme on points duty switched the traffic flow. 'I think I will also look for some nice present for Mr Palombo. He is a good man.'

'They're the ones who get hurt.' Cord glanced searchingly at the relaxed, almost sleepy figure by his side. 'Give those friends a message from me, Roder. Tell them that the way I see things it might help if there was some straight talking and fewer people playing at politics.'

'And this message, what should my friends do with it?' queried Roder innocently.

'Any damned thing they want,' said Cord heavily. 'They're your friends—not mine.'

He left the station wagon at the UNESCO office, saw it drive off, then went into the building. Maggie Delday's office was on the upper floor, a small room where the only feminine touch was a glass jar of mimosa blooms on top of a filing cabinet.

'Hello, Talos.' She stayed behind her desk, closing the file in front of her, sitting back, her smile wry at the edges. 'I heard what happened.'

'Whose version?'

'Tom Fielden first—he telephoned.' She took a cigarette from the plain wooden box beside her, lit it carefully with a bookmatch, and shrugged a little. 'Then Sunner came in. President Sharif has telegraphed an official protest to New York—copies to Rabat and the news agencies.'

He'd expected that, at least. 'How's Palombo?'

'No change that matters—he's still critical.' She ran a hand over her short, fair hair, the words weary. 'I'm planning to go back to the hospital as soon as I'm through here.'

Cord came round beside her and put his hands on her shoulders. He felt her relax beneath the light pressure of his fingers, and kept them there. 'Seen Mathilde Dolanne?'

The shoulders stiffened. 'No.'

'I only asked,' he said mildly. 'What about her Greeks? Are they still playing at tourists?'

'They're back, and she is on her way to Mihmaaz with Sharif—that's what Sunner said, anyway.' She looked around. 'You wanted me to do some spying . . .'

'Detective work,' he corrected firmly. 'Any luck?'

She nodded. 'Roder came here six weeks ago and said he'd worked for Bil-Maroc Oil at Tazzarine.'

'Six weeks. That means . . .'

'Just after Sharif arrived from Jemma to convalesce,' she agreed slowly, almost reluctantly. 'I called a man I know at Bil-Maroc. They've never heard of anyone called Roder.'

'Big surprise,' murmured Cord.

She frowned. 'That doesn't mean he wasn't with them. At plenty of these camps a stray Arab is just a cross on the weekly payroll.'

'Not the Roder variety.' Cord took his hands from her shoulders and seated himself on the edge of her desk. 'What about the other thing?'

'I checked that too. For whatever it matters, we've only two people who've had a tour of duty in Jemma. Joe Palombo was there for a time, about eight years back. The other one is Harry Peterley—he's our communications supervisor.' She opened the file in front of her. 'Here's his photograph.'

It was passport-sized and showed a stolid-looking heavy-faced man with thinning dark hair and a small moustache.

'How long since he was in Jemma?'

'About eighteen months—he was there with a medical aid team. Coming here was promotion. If you want to talk to him it'll have to wait until tomorrow. He's off duty now.' Maggie drew on the cigarette, watching him. 'Roder's one thing, Talos. But this . . .'

'Somebody's being fed information from here. Some of it isn't the kind Roder could lay his hands on easily,' he told her quietly. 'Is Peterley at the Affri?'

She shook her head. 'He says it costs too much. He

lives in an apartment of his own, not far from here.'

The address was in Avenue Sarg. Cord noted it and was left with another problem. 'When's Roder due off duty?'

'That's elastic, but usually around six.' She glanced at her watch. 'Right now he'll be at the transport pool garage—it's just round the corner. I could 'phone and have him come round.'

'That's rushing things.' Pensively, Cord gathered a handful of paper clips from a tin on the desk and began assembling them into a chain. 'Maggie, could you keep him working late? I need about an hour.'

She stubbed the half-smoked cigarette, frowned for a moment, then nodded. 'He could drive me to the hospital and wait to take me back to the Affri. Would that do?'

'Fine.' Cord grinned his thanks. 'Just make sure you give me that hour. Act naturally with him—as long as you do it'll be safe enough.'

'I'd like that in writing.' She grimaced ruefully, but reached for the telephone. 'I'll call him now. You—you'll be back later?'

'Sometime, Maggie,' he said carefully, laying down the completed chain of clips. 'But don't ask me when. It depends on a few things.'

.   .   .   .   .

Avenue Sarg was a street which boasted faded apartment blocks, close-parked cars and a pronounced smell of garbage—if not worse.

Cord paid off his cab at the corner and began to walk. Night had arrived and with darkness the temperature was beginning to fall. But a few shops were still open and further along a single café blazed with light. As he passed it, he heard an accordion playing off-key inside. The rest was like any street of its kind—a snatch of radio from one window, a woman shouting at her children, the occasional waft of cooking smoke.

Harry Peterley's address was the entrance to a narrow, ill-lit courtyard. He went through and stopped, frowning, feeling he'd landed in a rabbit-warren. All around flights of outside stairs led to doors in the upper floors. While Cord hesitated, an elderly, cognac-breathing Frenchman came down one of the stairways and headed towards the street. He stopped him and the man belched happily as he gave directions.

The third flight of stairs on the right, two up. Cord climbed the steps slowly, partly because he was still working out how he'd tackle Peterley, partly because the pain was once again gathering in his side.

The door had no nameplate and no bell. But there was a light burning behind it and he knocked, waited, and knocked again.

Nothing happened. Swearing softly, he tried the handle. It turned and the door opened a fraction. Cord looked into a short, plainly furnished hallway. Next moment he sensed as much as heard something happening behind him in the courtyard.

He looked round and down. There was a soft rustle of feet and a vague figure moved away, heading for the street.

Every alarm bell in his system began ringing. Palming the Neuhausen from his waistband he held it ready at hip level and used his other hand to ease the door wide. Three rooms led off the hallway, each with a beaded curtain in place of a door. The one furthest away had a light behind it.

His lips felt dry. He moistened them.

'Peterley?'

His voice echoed back, unanswered. Cord went in, let the door close behind him, and moved further down the hallway. Eyes and ears straining, he kept close to one wall, his attention fixed on the room at the end.

He was a yard from his goal when the sound—a whisper, nothing more—came from behind him. Out of the corner of his eye he caught a faint movement of the beaded curtain at the darkened room he'd just passed.

His reflexes took over, the responses drilled into him for years went into motion at the same instant as the muzzle of a short-barrelled revolver slipped into sight. Cord dived for the floor in a rolling twist, left hand gripping right wrist, the Neuhausen swinging into line.

The revolver fired first, an orange-tongued blast. He felt the wind of the bullet's passing, a second shot triggered wildly—then the Neuhausen bucked in his hand. Three shots in a vertical twelve-inch grouping. One below, one in line, one above the revolver's muzzle.

The beaded curtain convulsed. A heavy figure in a hooded Arab *djebba* pitched out and fell face-down, the revolver clattered across the floor. The man didn't move.

Cord got up, kicked the revolver aside, and checked the room. It held a bed and wardrobe. The wardrobe door hung open, its contents strewn around. The room next to it was a small, ill-kept kitchen.

That left the room where the light burned. It was Peterley's living room and the furnishings were heavy, old-fashioned colonial French. Again drawers were open, papers and clothes strewn around.

He began to move towards the window then stopped.

There was no need to look further for Harry Peterley. The man lay like a sack against the wall, naked, tied hand

and foot, a gag in his mouth. The gag didn't matter any more—not when that knife was stuck so deep in his chest.

But there had been more before that. The communications superintendent's face and body oozed blood from a score of smaller cuts, cuts placed with the careful sadism of an expert in pain.

Torture first, then death. For Peterley, it had probably come as something very close to unintended mercy.

A sick feeling in his throat, Cord forced himself to look again. The bloodied, slashed face was still twisted in a final death-agony. A tablecloth had been thrown from a drawer and was lying on the floor. With a sudden, irrational revulsion, he stooped, picked it up, and went to cover the man.

'Dead?' asked a quiet voice from behind him.

He dropped the tablecloth and was in the first stage of a crouching turn before the recognised the voice then saw its owner.

Major Rucos stood just inside the room. Behind the Moroccan stood a wide-eyed gendarme, machine-pistol at the ready.

Silently, Cord nodded. Rucos carefully pushed the gendarme's machine-pistol muzzle towards the floor then came over. As he looked for himself his hands clenched briefly, knuckle-tight, on his swagger cane. Rucos sighed, picked up the tablecloth himself, and draped it loosely over the body.

'The one in the hallway, Mr Cord?'

'Was waiting for me.' Cord drew a breath. 'Well, who uses a knife that way, major? Arab or Berber?'

Rucos's mouth snapped shut. Turning on his heel, he led the way into the hall, used a foot to roughly push the dead gunman on his side, then the tip of his swagger stick flicked the hood clear of the man's face. With a grunt of satisfaction he stood back.

'Neither, Mr Cord.'

The face was European, thin, clean-shaven, tanned, with mousey hair cut short. Under the native robe the man was clothed in a cheap, ill-fitting gabardine suit with a rumpled white shirt and a stringy black tie. All three of the Neuhausen's slugs had connected—one just below the ribs, one midway in the chest, the last high on the throat.

'Your kind.' There was a slight, sardonic inflection on the first word. Rucos gestured an invitation. 'If you want . . .'

Cord nodded, squatted down beside the body, and tackled the man's pockets. Rucos leaned against the wall.

'Why did you come here, Mr Cord?'

'To talk,' said Cord briefly. The inside pocket of the jacket yielded a few dirhans in notes. 'What about you?'

'The same.' Rucos hesitated a moment. 'There is little harm in saying it, and I would, of course, deny it elsewhere. Peterley was sometimes useful to me.'

'As your inside man at project headquarters?' Cord worked on. There was little in the final collection. A cheap watch, a plain gold ring on the left little finger, some spare ammunition for the revolver, two packs of cigarettes, a gun-metal lighter. Professionals seldom wore holes in their pockets. He sat back on his heels, waiting for an answer.

Rucos nodded. 'It is not wise to use the *tilifoon* for such matters. As always, I sent a man on ahead to make sure Peterly was alone—he saw you arrive and go in. Then we heard the shots.' His mouth shaped a fractional smile. 'I was not sure what to expect.'

'As long as you weren't disappointed.' Cord rose stiffly and went back into the living room. Ignoring Rucos for the moment he crossed to a table where there were bottles and glasses and poured himself a stiff measure of whisky. He drank it neat. It was raw, fiery stuff, probably made in someone's wash-boiler, but he needed it. 'How did Peterley land on your payroll?'

For once the Moroccan appeared uncomfortable. 'The man had—well, a certain weakness which brought him to my attention. There was an incident involving a child— he paid adequate compensation and the rest was a private, unofficial arrangement. As long as he behaved, as long as he gave me certain assistance . . .'

Cord nodded. It was nasty but practical and he didn't need the details spelled out.

'Did the thought ever strike you he could be feeding the same information to another customer?'

'I had this suspicion.' The words came flatly, unemotionally.

'He worked in Jemma for a time before he came here, major. Does that give you any ideas?'

'A few.' Rucos frowned and sought refuge in practicalities. 'I will have the house searched of course, but from its state that has been done already. And there is no saying that the man you killed did not have a companion who left earlier.' The blue eyes narrowed a little. 'For the moment a small fiction might be useful. If Peterley disturbed a burglar who killed him in a struggle . . .'

'And a gendarme shot the burglar as he tried to escape?' Cord saw benefits but there was a flaw. 'The neighbours might have a different story to tell.'

'In this street people have a singular lack of curiosity, usually with good reason.' Rucos wagged his stick in confident style. 'They will say nothing, Mr Cord. I can guarantee it.'

The truce between them was unspoken and wary. Cord suggested a look around the apartment. Rucos agreed, but never once left his side in the process. It yielded little beyond a collection of well-thumbed pornographic pictures, some crude enough to make even Rucos grunt in surprise. Whatever information Peterley had leaked there was no indication of its extent or who'd been on the receiving end.

The mortuary wagon arrived and Cord left. Outside, two gendarmes guarded the courtyard entrance. Beyond them, Avenue Sarg was strangely deserted. He flagged down a cruising cab, had it take him to the Affri, then told the driver to pull in and wait.

Exactly on seven p.m. the U.N. station wagon purred into sight. It drew up at the hotel, Maggie Delday got out, and as she headed into the brightly lit lobby the vehicle drew away.

Twenty dirhans in his pocket, another twenty promised, Cord's driver set the cab moving. Ahead of them, Roder took the direct route to the UNESCO block then swung down a side street and into a garage entrance at the rear. Cord had his driver carry on further down the street then stop.

Only minutes passed before Roder emerged from the garage. He looked around briefly, then began walking. The driver paid off, Cord left the cab and followed.

The slim figure ahead set a brisk pace. Within a short time broad avenues and bright lights gave way to narrow, crowded streets as the business area was left behind. Roder was heading deep into the old town, straight for the heart of the *suk*. Market stalls lined the way, busy with customers. Kerosene pressure lamps glowed over vast mounds of dates and grain, cheap pottery and canned goods.

Veiled women with shopping bags, young teenagers with transistor radios blaring, rattling old Renault trucks boring through the general hubbub—the world was a noisy, jostling place of strange odours and little patience. Cord closed the gap to a dangerous minimum in an effort to keep in sight of the bobbing woollen cap ahead—then just as quickly had to fall back as they reached a broad, open square.

It was a place where the old seemed to reign supreme—apart from a ramshackle array of buses and trucks parked to one side near a line of camels. Cooking fires burned on bare earth under the night sky. Bedouin from the south and Berber from the hills stalked and scowled amid a maze of black desert tents and more market stalls. Framed in the eerie green glare of naphtha flares, a trio of snake-charmers drummed up an audience while a couple of small boys grinned and sweated their way through a wild acrobatic dance routine.

'M'sieu . . .' a hand tugged Cord's sleeve. An eager, ragged Arab beckoned towards the show. 'One dirhan, you watch. Only three dirhans, you take pictures.'

Cord shook his head and brushed the tout aside. He saw Roder leaving the square, quickened his pace, and plunged into a new network of narrow streets. This was tourist territory—small shops which boasted windows, windows crammed with beaten silver and richly embossed leather.

'Maybe you buy nice handbag for lady?' The same ragged Arab had caught up again, grinning hopefully. 'I know best places, m'sieu.'

A glare and a wave repelled the man. Cord swung on again then stopped, swearing under his breath, no trace of Roder ahead. Then he gave a quick sigh of relief. His quarry had gone into a shop where most of the space seemed occupied by brass ornaments, miniature camel saddles and a jumble of other souvenir goods. A plump young shopkeeper in fez, shirt-sleeves and well-cut slacks was standing beside him, talking.

Roder nodded. Then, suddenly, deliberately, they both turned and grinned in Cord's direction.

'*M'sieu* . . .' the firm pressure of a pistol muzzle against his side brought Cord round slowly. The Arab tout's mouth was open in the same half-apologetic grin, but the eyes above were cold with menace. The pistol barrel nudged. '*Hinaak aho . . .*'

It needed no translation. Cord shrugged and allowed himself to be steered into the souvenir shop. The door closed behind them once they'd entered, the muzzle's pressure relaxed a little.

'Nice of you to look in, Mr Cord,' greeted Roder Hassabou with a grave politeness. 'We were hoping you'd do something like this.' He gave a twist of a smile. 'A couple of times I was scared you were going to lose me back there.' He glanced at his shirt-sleeved companion. 'All okay outside, Jusef?'

The man strolled to the door, looked out carefully, and nodded.

'Then round here.'

The gun prodded and Cord obeyed. They stopped behind a high mound of cushions and handwoven blankets. Expert hands patted over his clothes, Roder took the Neuhausen, then, without a word, the man in rags faded out of the shop.

'Now what?' asked Cord wearily. He had few illusions. Manner crisp, slouch vanished, this was a very different personality from the previous pose. The voice would have been enough on its own—the painfully constructed English had vanished, the new, mildly mocking accent was the one he'd heard the night before, blindfolded and against that wall. 'I'd say you've had your fun. So why not stop playing games?'

'Fun?' Roder showed a marked aversion to the word. 'Believe me, right now I'm pretty low on things to feel amused about—nothing personal. That's just how it is.'

Pushed along to a small door in the crumbling back wall, Cord was thumbed down a narrow, well-lit staircase. He went first, Roder following. At the bottom was a cellar which was part storeroom and part living quarters. Two men, young like the rest, both wearing oil-stained overalls, rose to their feet from beside a glowing stove. Roder greeted them with a nod.

'Mr Cord is visiting,' he said dryly. 'We should make him comfortable.'

They grinned, one produced a length of thin rope, and Cord's wrists were firmly tied in front. A knife flicked and the spare rope was used round each ankle, leaving him hobbled like a horse with a few inches of minimum movement.

'Sit down,' invited Roder.

The rope biting at each short step, Cord crossed to a packing case and perched on its edge. Roder looked at him for a moment, chuckled, laid down the Neuhausen, and lit a cigarette.

'You know who I am?' he asked suddenly.

Cord nodded. 'El Aggahr among other things. You made one or two mistakes along the way—so did Mathilde.'

'I know,' admitted Roder. A grimace crossed his high-cheeked, pock-marked face. 'But we're still amateurs in this business, whatever Mohammed Sharif thinks.' He started to tuck the cigarette pack away, changed his mind, and put one in Cord's mouth.

'Thanks.' Cord leaned forward for the light that followed then jerked his head towards the men in overalls. 'Either of them anywhere near Avenue Sarg tonight— Harry Peterley's home?'

Roder's mouth shaped distaste. 'No. Among other things, he serves too many masters.'

'He isn't serving any now. He's dead.'

'And you thought . . .' Roder sighed and shook his head. 'You still have things wrong, Mr Cord.'

'I didn't think you were involved,' said Cord carefully. 'But if you'd had a man there and he'd seen any visitors . . .'

'It might have helped you?' Relaxing, Roder settled himself on another of the boxes. 'We have helped when it seemed reasonable. For instance, you should have been friendlier to little Jali outside. He did his best to stop Sunner's man use that machine-pistol on your room.'

'Sunner's?' Somehow it didn't seem as much of a surprise as it should. 'You're sure?'

The query brought a slow, positive nod. 'Jali's knife is sharp. The man got away but it will be a long time before he recovers.'

'And by then you'll have finished off Sharif—the same way you nearly nailed Abdul Zieull at the power station.' Cord made it a flat statement of fact.

The thin lips opposite parted in a quizzical grin. Roder turned, translated quickly for his companions' benefit, and they chuckled. The taller of the two spat cheerfully against the stove, which gave a brief sizzle.

'Sharif we have plans for,' he agreed. 'But Abdul Zieull

—Mr Cord, even in Jemma a man seldom murders his own father. My mother, who is still his favourite wife, would tan my hide at the idea.'

'Zieull's your father?' Incredulously, trying to keep some semblance of grip on the situation, Cord stared at him. 'Then he's in on this?'

'No, and it was one hell of a job keeping out of sight while he was around today,' confessed Roder wryly. 'He thinks I'm in England, studying. London School of Economics, if you're interested. I didn't quite finish my course a few years back. Too much else to do—we had a protest march about something every week.'

'Nice for you,' grated Cord sardonically. 'But you're not protest marching this time.'

'We're not.' Roder's voice became serious. 'You know how things are. My country is in a mess, on the brink of war, people being butchered because they were born Mahhabi rather than Banu Khala—and I am Banu Khala, Mr Cord, in case it matters. There are plenty like me in Jemma, sickened of Sharif and what he stands for.' He sucked his cheeks into deep hollows of sad anger. 'El Aggahr means the hunter, but the title does not belong to any one man exclusively. Some of us have died, some— well, they vanished. But we are going to topple this Sharif.'

'The only way you'll do it is by killing him.' Cord eased back a little on the crate. 'The day it happens you'll start that war you're so worried about—and a whole lot more butchery.'

'There is another way.' Roder drew hard on his cigarette, dropped it half-smoked on the stone floor of the cellar, and crushed it underfoot. 'Sharif returns to Jemma soon. Before he steps off the 'plane he will be publicly

129

discredited, exposed for what he is. He will be arrested, tried, and probably executed—but legally. A caretaker government will be installed and elections held. The result is certain—a new, moderate government will negotiate an end to our troubles.'

'Then you'll live happily ever after,' said Cord dryly. 'Who'll do the arresting? Not your father—he's too busy howling for war with Daman.'

'He is still an honest man,' said Roder sharply. 'If we can present him with proof that Sharif is no better than a treacherous, money-grabbing snake he will act. And we will make sure the people also know the truth—that way, Sharif is finished.'

The door above opened. The shopkeeper looked down, murmured briefly, and one of the men in overalls hurried to join him. For a moment Roder hesitated then, as the door closed again, he asked bluntly, 'Have you told any-one what you know about Mathilde?'

'Not yet,' said Cord truthfully.

Roder eyed him steadily then nodded. 'Thank you for that—she is the one taking the real risks. You know she is half-Arab?'

'French father, Egyptian mother, that's how I heard it,' nodded Cord.

'That's also how Sharif heard it,' agreed Roder grimly. 'She was born in Egypt, but her mother was a Mahhabi from Jemma—a reasonably wealthy merchant family. Three years ago Mathilde's father died in a 'plane crash and her mother went back to Jemma.'

'And Mathilde?' Cord had a strange anticipation of the rest.

'By then she was in Europe, working as a model. Not long afterwards Sharif personally supervised a purge against some Mahhabi families—it turned attention from other troubles. A lot of people died, and one of them was Mathilde's mother—she was burned alive.' Quietly, dispassionately, he fanned his hands in a silent explanation of the rest. 'Mathilde came back. Her first plan was simply to get close to Sharif and kill him. But—well, some friends persuaded her there had to be a better way.'

'So she lives with Sharif.' Cord saw the words bring a quick flicker of pain and guessed why. 'You just let it happen?'

'You think it was my idea?' The thin face twisted bitterly. 'She shaped her own way and she waits—just as a lot of other people have waited. But when Sharif came here we knew our chance was coming—because we already knew why Sharif has to get your U.N. power and water project.'

'To help swing the mineral rights deal,' murmured Cord. He took another two-handed puff on the cigarette. 'What about it, Roder—how much of this rutile deposit is over the border in Daman?'

Roder stared at him, then his breath came out like an explosion. 'You work fast—faster than I guessed!' He got up, walked the narrow length of the cellar and back, then stopped beside his captive. 'We're not sure. Mathilde's guess is around thirty per cent in Jemma, the main deposit over on the Daman coastal strip. Sharif is offering this syndicate the kind of deal they can't refuse provided they use Jemma as their base.'

'While he rigs his own crisis to get the lot,' said Cord softly. 'And the attempts on his life?'

'What attempts, so far?' demanded Roder. 'Atalan Said is killed in New York—Mohammed Sharif will hardly miss him. This afternoon's bomb? Sharif refused to go on the tour. My father was near the front, Captain Sunner well back, and a radio-mine transmitter can fit anyone's pocket. My guess is Sunner was too concerned for his own safety and pressed the button early.'

It made sense, admitted Cord—accepting the stakes involved. He stubbed his cigarette on the crate.

'Then why the hints that Sharif was in danger?'

'Because things have happened which worry us.'

'Like the cockerel heads?'

'No.' Roder spared a fractional smile. 'Mathilde planted the one at Mihmaaz, I did your own. We wanted to have you on guard, to make sure you helped us keep Sharif alive the way we need him. But other people have been spying around the valley, getting past the Moroccan outposts.'

'You've seen them?' Cord flexed his wrists, cursing the ropes.

Roder grimaced. 'Worse. Twice we have almost collided with them. And Mathilde says Sunner is strangely on edge—as if he knows something of which even Sharif is unaware.'

Cord remembered the microphone bug at the airport but steered round to what mattered most. 'You say there's evidence which will topple Sharif. The rutile deal? Because pulling a fast one on Daman is more likely to leave him looking like a hero.'

'Money,' said Roder shortly. 'Sharif could have imposed tougher terms on the Greeks and still left the proposition ridiculously attractive. He has not tried. And Pauol, their senior man, has been out twice before on his own. When Pauol was at the valley only Sharif and Sunner saw him—even Mathilde was kept out. But Mathilde knows something was signed, a secret agreement. An additional benefit, direct to Sharif . . .'

'A chunk of money into a Swiss bank account.' Cord whistled his appreciation. 'All the best presidents have their pension fund. You think you can prove it?'

'We must,' said Roder calmly. 'And we know where to look.'

The door above opened again and the fat, swarthy shopkeeper ambled down. He looked at Roder and nodded.

'Time to go,' said Roder quietly. The remaining man in overalls handed him a leather jacket then stooped to pick up a small, canvas-wrapped bundle. Roder shrugged into the jacket, zipped it together at the front, and slipped a Luger pistol into one pocket. He glanced at Cord's Neuhausen then handed it to the shopkeeper. 'Jusef, you will take good care of our guest.'

'You haven't a hope in that valley,' said Cord hoarsely, struggling to his feet. 'You can't burgle that place and get away with it.'

'One man can get through where more would fail,' said Roder with a small smile. 'And Mathilde expects me. We will find our proof. I have a little camera, a Japanese model—it will take pictures by the light of a match. I take my pictures, I get out again and nothing is disturbed.'

'You're crazy.' Cord sighed then on an impulse held out his wrists. 'Look, cut me loose and I'll come along.'

Roder shook his head. 'No. I trust you, Talos Cord— perhaps because there is something strange about you I only half understand. But you stay.'

Cord sank back on the crate, knowing it was useless. 'Then good luck—you'll need it.'

The man in overalls was waiting at the top of the steps. Roder pulled the woollen cap a little lower on his forehead and gave a wry half-salute.

'*Bellafia* . . . goodbye for now, Talos. Allah willing, I will eat breakfast with you.'

He left and the door slammed shut. The shopkeeper met Cord's eyes, shrugged, and turned away.

A moment later an engine started up somewhere outside. The vehicle grated into gear and rumbled away. As the sound faded, Cord looked down at the rope on his wrists and felt almost glad he'd been turned down.

Roder Hassabou Zieull was heading straight into a den of pitiless killers—with little more than blind courage to back him up.

7

There were rats in the cellar. Talos Cord heard their quick scurrying feet and occasional squeals as the long, tense night dragged on. Always cautious, moderately friendly, his two gaolers took turn about at watching and sleeping. The electric light burned throughout and the pile of old, smelly mats given him as a bed housed a voracious variety of flea.

Jusef took first spell of duty. The fat shopkeeper made coffee on a spirit stove, gave his prisoner a cup, and settled on a chair a few feet away. By then, Cord had investigated the thin rope round his wrists and feet and had reluctantly dismissed any thoughts of wriggling loose from those tight, expert knots. He tried talking to the man, but got nowhere. When Jali took over it was the same. Jali only grinned.

Eventually, around midnight, Cord fell asleep. Twice he woke, conscious that the men were changing over, hearing their low-voiced conversation. But the next time a hand was shaking his shoulder.

'*Saha, Ingliizi* . . . wake up.' Jusef frowned down at him.

Yawning, he twisted round and glanced at his watch. It was eight a.m. As his brain came to life he looked round the cellar, then back to the shopkeeper.

'Roder?'

Slowly, uneasily, Jusef shook his head.

'No word?'

'Nothing.' The man's thick lips pursed briefly. 'There could be many reasons.'

'Like hell.' Cord elbowed himself upright on the mats. 'If he isn't back there's only one answer—and you know it. Sharif got him.' He held out his wrists. 'Cut me loose.'

Slowly, Jusef shook his head. 'You stay. Roder will come. And we have no customers to worry about upstairs. This is the day of prayer—this shop is always closed on Fridays.'

Protests were useless. Taken briefly from the cellar, he was allowed to wash in a small bathroom at the rear of the shuttered shop then was brought back to the cellar. Jali had more coffee and coarse native bread waiting.

The day crept on. By noon the two Arabs were openly glum. By mid-afternoon they were despondent. Weary of trying to persuade them, Cord smoked the last of his cheroots and said nothing. At last, as his wristwatch ticked round to six p.m., the two men went into a sudden, low-voiced huddle. Finally Jusef nodded, rose, and came over.

'*Ingliizi* . . .' voice dull, the man reached into the pocket of his slacks. When his hand came out there was the soft click of a spring-blade. Cord stared at the knife then relaxed with a half-suppressed sigh as it was laid on the cellar floor just out of his reach.

'It is as Roder asked,' said Jusef quietly, his eyes holding a sad acceptance. '*Salaam aleekum*, Mr Cord. We will leave now. This shop'—he shrugged—'it has served its purpose.'

'I'll find out what I can about Roder,' said Cord softly, nodding his understanding. 'But later I might need help —maybe your kind of help. So why not stay? There'll be no police, I promise it. And it would mean I could make contact with your people.' He saw the man hesitate, undecided, and added with a slow emphasis, 'Roder said he could trust me. That means you can.'

For another long moment Jusef stood silent, frowning. Then he nodded.

The ropes cut away, it was a full five minutes before Cord managed to rub the last of the cramp from his wrists and ankles. Then he was ready to go. Jusef solemnly returned the Neuhausen then went on ahead to open the door at the top of the steps.

.   .   .   .   .

Outside the shop it was nearing dusk. A few doors along a cab had just unloaded a tourist family and he flagged it down as it began to move off. Cord climbed aboard, told the driver to take him to the Affri, then slumped back on the cracked, worn upholstery and wondered exactly where to begin.

He'd lost near enough a full day, a day in which nearly anything could have happened, in which any number of things could have changed. Only one fact was crystal clear. Roder and the two men who'd gone with him had hit trouble at Mihmaaz valley. The odds were heavy against any of them being still alive. Come to that, Mathilde's prospects were almost equally bleak.

Heavy cross-town traffic made it a slow trip to the hotel. When the cab finally halted he thrust some money at the driver, hurried up the entrance steps, and headed straight towards the reception desk.

'M'sieu Cord!' The desk clerk greeted him with undisguised relief. 'You had us worried. The telephone message you would be away was so—ah—unusual.'

'Message?' Cord blinked, understood, and quickly nodded. Roder had obviously paid attention to detail. 'Everything's fine. Anyone been looking for me?'

The answer was an expressive eyebrow. Rapidly, the clerk began counting off on his fingers. 'There was Major Rucos, most anxiously. Then M'sieu Jackson and Madame Delday . . .'

Cord cut him short. 'Are they here?'

'Non.' The clerk sniffed. 'Like you they have had to go off on some urgent business.' He peered closer, showing a slight distaste. 'You have need of a shave, m'sieu? We have an excellent barber.'

'It can wait. First of all, I want . . .' Cord's voice died away. The main door had swung open. Through it in a noisy, laughing cluster came the four Interlak Corporation negotiators. In the lead, grinning from ear to ear and carrying a briefcase, the bald-headed Pauol was a transformation of the stolid, humourless individual he'd seen before.

Leaving the clerk, he crossed the lobby towards them.

'Ah, Mr Cord!' Pauol greeted him with an expansive gesture of delight. Behind him, the others came to a ragged halt. One swayed slightly and hiccuped. 'Tonight you will drink with us—we will toast your United Nations, our company, and the Democratic Republic of Jemma. Long may we all prosper!'

'Sharif signed?' He could smell liquor on their breath, guessed the celebration was already under way.

'The agreement is here—signed, witnessed, sealed, complete.' Pauol slapped the briefcase hard. 'Our task is done. Tomorrow we go home—tonight we enjoy ourselves.'

The words brought another noisy chorus of agreement.

'How long since you left the valley?' demanded Cord.

Pauol managed to look slightly sheepish. 'Some little time—early afternoon, to be truthful. There was this little bar in this village, we had hired our own car and a driver.' He screwed his face into a wink and pressed a hand to his glistening, sun-reddened head. 'Already I have a feeling this will be a night to remember.'

'That's likely,' said Cord unemotionally. 'How were things at the valley? Did they mention any trouble?'

'Trouble? No.' Pauol glanced round. Two of the Greeks were already on their way to the bar. The third was hovering impatiently. 'Now you come with us, eh?'

'Maybe later.' Cord started to swing away then stopped. 'Was Mathilde there?'

'That one'—Pauol smacked his lips—'now that, my friend, is a beautiful piece of woman.'

'Was she there?'

Almost sadly, the man shook his head. 'There, yes— but we did not see her. The president said she had some sickness in the stomach.' He grew suddenly confidential. 'In these countries there is only one answer, Mr Cord. Never drink water without wine. Better still, drink only wine.'

Laughing at his own joke, Pauol headed after the

others. Cord stayed where he was for a moment, gnawing his lip, knowing the desk clerk was watching him, saying what came close to a silent prayer for Mathilde Dolanne if her 'sickness' meant what he thought.

Abruptly, he turned on his heel and headed out again. The usual line of taxis was waiting outside. He signalled, the lead driver cruised forward and greeted him with a questioning grin.

'M'sieu?'

'The U.N. building.' Cord climbed aboard, turning a deaf ear to the man's cheerful, gossiping chatter as the cab threaded its way.

The agreement was signed. Mohammed Sharif was fully committed. He wondered how much the man's private rake-off might be. A million, two million, more? When bribery reached international scale the sky could be the limit.

.　　　.　　　.　　　.　　　.

Talos Cord's arrival at the UNESCO offices beat the main door's closing for the night by a matter of seconds. The remaining senior assistant, a crew-cut Austrian named Weigel, turned back to his office with a wry nod and a shade of reluctance.

'We wondered what happened to you.' He flipped open a box on his desk and offered Cord one of the thin, eight-inch black cigars it contained. 'Wondered maybe isn't the right word—Maggie Delday had some crazy idea you'd been knocked on the head and slung across a camel or worse.' He struck a match and held it till Cord had the cigar going properly. 'Still, with what has happened who'd blame her? You've heard about last night—about Peterley?'

Cord nodded. 'How's Joe Palombo?'

'Doing fine. Still flat on his back, but starting to give orders.' Weigel's chuckle indicated this was to be expected. 'He'd like to see you.'

'And I'd like to see Walt Jackson or Maggie,' said Cord grimly. 'The clerk at the Affri said they'd headed off somewhere. When are they due back?'

Weigel scratched his head. 'I wish I knew. Cord, this has been one of those days. As if we hadn't enough going wrong, one of our best drivers—Roder, the one you had yesterday—walks out on us without even turning up to wave goodbye. Then we hit labour trouble at the erosion project. No sooner do we seem to have that smoothed than Walt and Maggie decide to head off for Mihmaaz . . .'

'The valley'—Cord stared at him in dismay—'why?'

Weigel shrugged, vaguely surprised. 'I thought maybe you'd know. We had a signal from New York, personal from the Secretary General to be delivered to President Sharif. Walt's our senior man for the moment, so he said he'd be postman. Maggie—well, somebody had to drive him and she volunteered. So they 'phoned Mihmaaz to say they were coming then headed there.'

Cord gave a long sigh. 'When did they leave?'

'Three hours ago, maybe more. Time enough to get there and back, that's for sure.' The Austrian frowned, with troubles of his own. 'Now there's more trouble at the erosion project and we've a strike on our hands. Walt Jackson could sort it out, but nobody else—and there's damn all we can do till he gets back.'

'You've tried telephoning the valley?'

'Tried,' emphasised Weigel. 'This is Morocco, Mr Cord. The *tilifoon* has off-moments. The switchboard say they can't get a call through—something's happened to the line.' The man grimaced. 'Probably means some Arab ran short of fencing wire.'

'Not this time.' Cord rose to his feet, a chill sense of urgency running through him. 'Weigel, I've got to get up there. I'll need a car.'

Weigel frowned but nodded. 'I can fix it. You—well, you think they're in trouble?'

'Trouble they can't handle. What was in the signal from New York?'

'Nothing much the way I read it.' Worried now, Weigel moistened his lips. 'Official regrets for yesterday's business at the power station, the usual line about the need to strive for peace.'

'Any mention of boundary negotiations?'

Weigel shook his head and Cord relaxed a fraction. Field Reconnaissance usually kept the lid on its information until the facts were watertight, but now and again it could happen.

The telephone on Weigel's desk began ringing. The Austrian swore apologetically, lifted it, and answered. He listened for a moment then put his hand over the mouthpiece.

'We've a visitor. Major Rucos—looking for you. He knows you're here.'

'Say I'll be right along.' He waited while Weigel repeated the message and grinned a little as the receiver went down. Just this once Rucos was the one man he needed. 'Forget that car. I'm going to have company.'

The cigar box was still open. He glanced significantly from the box to its owner, saw him nod, and helped himself to a handful. Then he went out, leaving the Austrian still shaking his head in troubled bewilderment.

.   .   .   .   .

Rucos was waiting impatiently at the main door, tight-lipped, his thin moustache twisted in a scowl of displeasure. It hardened further when he saw Cord coming along towards him.

'At last. *Ya salaam* ... Cord, until five minutes ago when the Affri desk clerk telephoned me, I have had a full-scale search in progress for you. You walk out into the night and—and ...'

'Vanish?' Cord nodded. 'It happened that way.'

'And now I want to know why,' began Rucos. The swagger stick beat a light, rapid tattoo against his side. 'There has been trouble, effort ...'

'Keep it for later.' Cord ignored the small man's splutter of indignation. 'Right now I need your help—and maybe you need mine. You've still got that radio link to your guard post at Mihmaaz?'

The words ready on Rucos's lips died. He looked at Cord for a moment, seemed to read what he saw there, and gave a short, questioning nod.

'Call them up,' said Cord grimly. 'Ask them when a U.N. car entered the valley this afternoon—and find out if it has left.'

'Outside.' Rucos led the way in the gathering darkness. He had a jeep parked at the kerb, a tall radio aerial at its tail. As they climbed aboard he explained, 'I can't reach direct, but Headquarters will relay.'

Cord watched as the Moroccan flicked switches and spoke curtly into the microphone. An acknowledgement crackled back.

'It will take a minute.' A scowl came back into Rucos's voice. 'You think something is wrong out there? The Greeks are back—they seemed happy, or so I am told.'

'They should be.' Cord stared at the radio, willing it to

life again. 'Did your people report anything happening in the valley last night—any kind of panic?'

A strange expression, part shadowed suspicion, part concern, crossed the Moroccan's face in the glow of the street lamps. '*Aywa* . . . they did. Shots were fired. Our posts went on the alert. We sent men to investigate. They were turned back, told that someone had been drinking too much and played the fool with a gun. Later, Sunner himself apologised.'

'You believe it?'

'No.' The word came flatly, with an underlying disgust. 'But can I call them liars?'

'Three men went into the valley last night,' said Cord quietly. 'They didn't come back.'

'Your men?' Rucos stiffened a little then as quickly dismissed the proposition. 'No. I think you would have been with them. Who were they?'

'El Aggahr's people. Two of their pals kept me trussed in a cellar then—well, let me go when they gave up hope.'

Leaning forward, Rucos switched on the hooded dashboard light. 'Your wrists. Hold them out.'

Cord did. The ropemark weals showed plain under the shaded gleam. The Moroccan grunted his acceptance.

'The three men. They planned to kill Sharif?'

'No. That's not what they want. They went in to find something.' He let Rucos work out the rest any way he chose. 'How much longer will this radio link need?'

'We should have heard by now.' Rucos scooped up the microphone and tried again. The loudspeaker maintained a low background crackle of static for a few seconds then he was answered in a crisp unemotional burst of Arabic.

'Well?' queried Cord.

Rucos ignored him, raised the microphone again,

rapped a query, was answered, and appeared startled. His hand tightened round the microphone. '*Yalla . . .*' he spoke quickly, emphatically for a few seconds then closed the switch and stared at the set, an expression of concerned disbelief on his face.

'Major?' Cord tried again.

Slowly, Rucos shook his head. 'No answer, Cord. They have been called and called again—but there is no answer. District Headquarters has heard nothing from them since the schedule call at sixteen-thirty hours. Another schedule call was due half-an-hour ago.'

Suddenly, savagely, he key-started the jeep and revved the engine hard. Their eyes met, each with the same unspoken thought. Then Rucos rammed the jeep into gear, and they got under way.

·   ·   ·   ·   ·

As a journey it took on nightmare character. Thin, sharp-featured face a mask, hands knuckle-tight on the wheel, Rucos drove with a harsh, icy purpose and the accelerator most of the time on the boards. Up front, between the glaring headlamps, the winking red of the jeep's priority warning light cleared all traffic from their path.

Clinging to the passenger grab handle, the night wind plucking and battering his clothes, Cord shut his eyes a dozen times a mile as hazards loomed towards them. Dark, anonymous figures scurried to the safety of the verges. Vehicles swung frantically off the road—one truck slammed axle-deep into a ditch in its driver's panic. As a demonstration of the power of the red light of authority it was impressive. But the rest was terrifying . . . and one glance at Rucos would have made it plain to anyone he was relying absolutely on the winking signal.

A fresh, tortured squeal of rubber marked the moment when they branched off and took the mountain road. Now there was no traffic but if anything the rest was worse. Each hairpin turn and eroded edge held a new dimension of danger in that blue velvet night, a night with stars like crusted diamonds and a sickly, overhanging crescent of moon so near it might have been there to touch.

The jeep bounced and jolted, tossed them from their seats, at times leaving Rucos clinging monkey-like to the wheel with his body apparently in mid-air. The head-lamps cast new, deeper shadows and began glinting on the first patches of snow. It grew steadily colder, till even the road surface showed the gathering silvered traces of night frost.

Then, just as suddenly, it was over. Rucos dropped a gear, took the jeep onto the short length of secondary track for Mihmaaz valley, and moments later braked the jeep to a halt, headlamps still blazing.

The guard-post lay ahead, its barrier pole raised. To one side the same army jeep lay parked beside the small cluster of bivouac tents. Nothing moved, no one appeared to challenge them. Moistening his lips, Rucos switched off the engine and killed the red warning light.

Still nothing moved, the only sound was the soft mournful whisper of the mountain wind.

But they were not completely alone. Gradually, Cord's eyes began to pick out detail. A khaki-clad figure lay in a motionless huddle to the right, where the heavy machine-gun was dug in. Another khaki shape lay face-down beside the patrol jeep, one arm still upraised, hand hooking against the driver's seat.

For the space of a few heart-beats Major Rucos sat

like a figure carved from stone. Then, as Cord made to swing out of the jeep, the spell which held him ended. Wordlessly, he pulled a torch from under the dashboard and handed it to Cord. Reaching behind him, he opened a locker and dragged out a short-barrelled automatic carbine.

They went to the dug-in machine-gun first. Cord squatted beside the dead soldier, switched on the torch, then glanced up at Rucos. The man's throat had been cut, the gun's safety lock was still on, the signs were he'd died almost without knowing it.

He heard Rucos draw a long, tortured breath.

'Ten men, Cord—there were ten here.' The Moroccan's voice quivered then steadied. 'Good men, hand-picked.' Suddenly he spun round and headed at a run towards the bivouac tents. Cord rose slowly and followed.

Every man of the guard-post detail was dead, their bodies scattered where they'd fallen. All but one seemed to have been taken by surprise, killed by a single blow by knife or bayonet. The sole exception, a man with corporal's stripes on his uniform blouse, was the soldier who had almost reached the patrol jeep. He was unarmed and his feet were bare. His skull had been crushed by a rifle butt. On the ground nearby lay a dark blue uniform beret. Cord lifted it and pointed silently to the flash of green and gold ribbon sewn to one side. It was identification enough.

'Sunner's gangsters.' Naked hatred in the words, Rucos glared into the dark beginnings of the valley track. 'They will be far away by now.'

Dry-lipped, Cord nodded. An attack soon after dusk tied in with the sudden radio silence, and would mean nearly two hours had passed since the massacre. The wind murmured again, ice-edged from the high country, and he shivered despite himself.

'It makes no sense, none I can understand,' muttered Rucos with something close to anguish in his voice. '*Ma bafham* ... why, Cord? Tell me that.'

'Mohammed Sharif.' It seemed the only possible answer. Cord scraped a hand along his unshaven jaw-line, building thoughts on the name. 'There's a lot of money being carved in different directions because of what's happening in Jemma. Maybe Sunner has his own ideas about sharing it out.' He clicked off the torch to conserve the battery. 'What about the other guard-posts?'

Rucos froze for a moment at the reminder. 'There are four—small ones, of three men each, on the hill tracks. They had—they have short-range walkie-talkie links with here. We can try them.'

The patrol jeep's radio they found smashed—perhaps by the same rifle butt. There was still their own vehicle's transmitter. Rucos feverishly spun the dials, adjusted frequencies and began calling.

The first thin, heavily distorted reply crackled back within seconds. Then, in turn, the other posts reported in. As the last voice ended Rucos sank back with a grunt of relief.

'All safe. They know nothing, except that their calls have been unanswered.'

'It figures,' agreed Cord grimly. 'This is the only road, the way Sunner had to come—but he's too clever to pick unnecessary trouble. You'll bring them down here?'

'And contact Marrakech,' said Rucos purposefully. 'A general alert—we will find these devils, Cord. My word as a Berber on that.' It was no idle promise, and there would be little mercy for any of Sunner's men who came the way of that small, determined figure.

Cord nodded. 'While you do that I'll take a look up at the house. Right?'

Pursing his lips, Rucos handed him the carbine. 'Take this—just in case. I will follow before long.'

He swung back to the radio. Cord turned up the thin cloth of his jacket collar against the wind, slung the carbine over one shoulder and began walking.

.   .   .   .   .

Five minutes later Talos Cord stood at the end of the pass, looked out across the mountain-fringed stretch of Mihmaaz valley, and swore softly.

What he could see had all the appearance of peaceful normality. Lights burned behind the chalet windows. He could hear music coming from a radio. The glinting black shape of Sharif's armour-plated Rolls-Royce was parked conspicuously in front of the main verandah.

All the night scene lacked was a glimpse of people. And as he moved forward, feet crunching on the gravel-like soil, he heard a murmur of voices from the nearest of the outbuildings.

Tight-lipped, the carbine ready, he crossed over and peered round the edge of a narrow slit of lighted window. Then he relaxed. Inside, a dozen or so native servants were clustered in a wan, frightened group round a wood stove. He found the entrance door, saw the way it was locked and barred, and decided to leave them there till later.

Heading for the chalet next, he came across the U.N. station wagon drawn into a patch of deep shadow. He gave it a glance then shrugged and went on.

At the top of the steps the chalet's front door lay wide open. He walked unchallenged down the long corridor past empty rooms, the radio music growing louder. The radio was behind another open door. Cord went in, switched it off, and was back in the corridor when a new, muffled sound reached his ears.

It came again, a half-shout, half-moan from somewhere to the right. He found a short side-passage, and tried the door at the end. It was locked, but as he rattled the handle the call came again.

One kick smashed the lock. On the other side a small, bare storeroom was in darkness. Cord found the light switch, the bulb overhead flared to life—and he winced.

Three dead men lay side by side on the stone-flagged floor. Two were the Arabs who'd been with Roder. The other, a European, wore the dark blue battledress of Sunner's mercenaries.

'Over here, Talos Cord.' The voice, racked with pain, brought him round.

Shoulders propped against a cupboard door, body drawn up tight on the floor, one bloodstained hand pressing hard against his stomach, Roder Hassabou Zieull's face was a battered, bloodied mask. But he still managed to force something resembling a smile.

Cord bent over him, put down the carbine, and reached to remove Roder's hand. The young Arab shook his head.

'Let it stay. It holds life in—I have told myself that for three hours now.' He ran his tongue over smashed lips. '*Moya* . . . some water would help.'

There was a sink and tap in the corner opposite but no sign of a cup. Cord found an empty glass jam jar, half filled it, and let Roder sip for a moment.

'What happened?' he asked almost mechanically.

Roder spoke weakly but calmly. 'Captain Sunner ordered my—my disposal before they left. His sergeant

149

does not believe in a clean kill.' His eyes, mere slits in swollen, puffy tissue, met Cord's. 'It—it is almost fortunate that a bullet in the—the stomach makes such a slow way to die.'

'Wait.' Cord picked up the carbine, smashed the glass of the storeroom window with the barrel, and fired three spaced shots into the night air. 'Rucos is down the pass— he can radio for an ambulance. They wiped out the main guard-post but left the others.'

Roder nodded his understanding then twisted a grimace. 'Talos, you were right and I was wrong. Sunner's guards were—they were too efficient.' He turned his eyes briefly towards the bodies on the floor then looked away. 'I was in the sun-lounge, at the desk with Mathilde when —when the shooting began outside. There was no time, no chance. Mathilde—she had a little pistol. I made her point it at me and shout for—for help.'

He clenched his teeth and closed his eyes for a moment, breathing in quick, shallow gasps. Quickly, Cord moistened his lips again with the water.

'Easy,' he encouraged softly. 'It won't be long. We'll get you back to Marrakech. Maybe you'll land in the next bed to Joe Palombo.'

'*Inshallah* . . . but I will tell the rest quickly.' Roder looked at him again, nodding his thanks for the try. 'I— they question thoroughly, but I said little. Sunner suspected Mathilde and had her guarded—Sharif did not like that. Then I—I heard the Greeks arrive.'

'The contracts are signed,' said Cord. 'They went back to Marrakech. What about Walt Jackson and Maggie?'

Roder shook his head. 'I know only that they came here after Sunner seized Sharif. They were'—he stopped, fresh beads of sweat running down from his forehead, streaking through the blood—'they were unlucky, but they are alive.'

'Where did he take them?' Cord leaned over him, intent on the answer. 'Roder, do you know?'

The faint sound of a vehicle engine reached his ears. Major Rucos was on his way. Roder heard it too. Breathing faster, his voice gained a new, desperate urgency.

'I heard Sunner talk of—of some place called Zinaad. It was when he told Sergeant Denke to finish me.' He struggled up a little on his elbows as the sound of the approaching jeep came closer. 'Talos, I—I found that agreement, the secret clause. But there was no time to photograph it. The little camera—it—I hid it in the room, in that couch. You will use it and—do the rest?'

Slowly, Cord nodded.

'Good.' It came like a sigh. Roder sank back, his relief plain. 'Then get it to my father. He—he will understand.'

The jeep stopped outside. In another moment footsteps sounded in the corridor. Cord turned, shouted, and Major Rucos arrived in a matter of seconds. He stood in the doorway, paid scant attention to the three dead men, but gave a quick frown as he saw Roder.

'I know this one,' he said accusingly. 'He was Jackson's driver.'

'Among other things, major.' Roder answered for himself, his eyes closed again, his voice little more than a whisper. 'They are at a place called Zinaad. You—you know it?'

'Zinaad?' Rucos drew a hissing, surprised intake of breath. 'I know it, yes.'

Cord swung on the Moroccan. 'He needs an ambulance, fast. Better still, that helicopter.'

'The ambulance, yes. But no helicopter could risk these

mountains by night,' said Rucos positively. 'Stay with him. I will make the call.'

He went out again, his quick footsteps fading.

'The camera'—Roder inched up again, forcing the words out—'now, Talos. Get it.'

Cord hesitated, saw the desperate plea in the young eyes, and nodded. He left the storeroom, reached the heavy, carved door of the chalet's main lounge, saw the desk with its drawers hanging open and empty, and went straight over to the couch—the same couch where he'd seen Mohammed Sharif lolling in state.

Time was short. He threw the cushions aside, found the tiny camera jammed down the back, rammed it in his pocket, and was turning to go when a glint of steel caught his eye above the big, open fireplace.

Driven deep into the carved wood of the mantelshelf, a bayonet pinned its way through a sealed white envelope, an envelope with his name on the front. Cord wrenched the weapon free, used its point to slit the envelope, and dragged out the single sheet inside.

The message was from Sunner, written in a neat, rounded, schoolmasterish hand.

I will make appropriate arrangements for the release of Mohammed Sharif on payment of the sum of two million dollars. This sum is assessed on worth and should cause minimal embarrassment to interested parties.

Details regarding payment will follow. Any public announcement or attempt to trace or hinder our movements will cause the immediate death of two U.N. staff.

He threw the bayonet aside and headed back to the storeroom, the note still in his hand, a chill sense of Sunner's absolute ruthlessness overcoming everything in his mind. Then, when he reached the storeroom, he stopped short in the doorway. Rucos was back, standing in the middle of the floor, lighting a cigarette, glancing at him with a faint reproach.

'I asked you to wait,' said Rucos almost conversationally. 'Now—well, I can cancel the ambulance. The man is dead.'

Cord pushed past him. Roder's head had fallen to one side. The hand which had pressed so faithfully against the round hole of the bullet-wound in his stomach lay clear now, palm up as if in a final gesture of hope. There was no pulse.

'A man can live only so long, even with a purpose,' murmured Rucos thoughtfully. He took a long, slow puff on the cigarette. 'Who was he, Cord?'

'Someone I liked.'

'Yet you left him.' The Moroccan raised an eyebrow in grim, questioning fashion. 'Why?'

Instead of answering, Cord held out the note. 'I found this.'

The cigarette dangling from his lips, Rucos read Sunner's message in a slow, frowning concentration. The colour was back in the thin, brown cheeks again, the blue eyes were cold and hard and speculative.

'Two *milyoon*—is any politician worth so much?'

'Sharif is, to several people,' said Cord almost irritably. He considered the soldier silently. Rucos opened his mouth to speak again then saw his face and stopped, waiting.

'Major, can you be two people at once?' asked Cord.

'*Kaam* . . . how many?' Rucos blinked in surprise.

'I might tell someone what's been happening—if that someone wasn't in Moroccan security while he listened.'

'I understand.' Rucos took a last, lingering draw on his

cigarette, dropped it on the floor, and looked very deliberately at his wristwatch. 'The paths down from the mountain are not easy. It will be another ten minutes before these men arrive.' He shrugged and smiled faintly. 'If it interests you, my given name is Haran.'

It was Cord's turn to nod his understanding.

He began as near the beginning as was necessary and talked quickly, capsuling details, leaving out few of the essentials.

Rucos was a good listener. He sucked his teeth in surprise a few times but said nothing until Cord finished.

'It would help if there was more proof of these things,' he frowned at last. 'No'—he forestalled Cord's protest— 'I am not challenging their truth. Not now. And if I had known earlier, what could I have done anyway?'

'Very little the way I see it,' said Cord grimly. 'It wasn't your job.'

'But it is now.' Rucos scratched sadly along his moustache then glanced back into the room. 'And there we have El Aggahr—that one, at least, I had never suspected. What was his real name?'

'It can keep for now.'

'Then we should leave here.' Rucos gestured towards the door, saw Cord hesitate, and added quietly. 'The dead can always wait. But not the living.'

. . . . .

Another radio call from the jeep advised Marrakech to cancel the ambulance. Rucos added some fresh instructions then replaced the microphone as the first wary, panting soldiers from the hill outposts arrived at a weary jog-trot.

They were twelve in all. Rucos detailed them to a

variety of immediate tasks, from freeing and questioning the servants in the outhouse block to standing sentry at the scene of the guard-post massacre.

When he'd finished, only one man remained on the verandah. He was a spindle-shanked, hawk-faced private who twitched a suspicion of a grin as Rucos finally beckoned him over.

'This one is a Berber, as I am,' said Rucos with a quiet satisfaction. 'His name is Ahmad—we come from the same village, when the French were here we hid together in these mountains. And he knows where Zinaad is—as I do.'

He turned away, entering in a quick, low-voiced conversation with the soldier. Cord waited with an attempt at patience, lighting one of the long, thin cigars he'd borrowed back in Marrakech, wondering at the delay. Whatever was going on, it was no officer to enlisted man discussion. Though their voices stayed low, the two men argued hard at times with Ahmad throwing him the occasional doubtful glance.

At last, Rucos nodded and the soldier ambled off.

'Settled it?' asked Cord dryly.

'You might say that.' Rucos coughed lightly. 'We had different viewpoints. Cord, how many men would you say are with Sunner?'

He shrugged. 'I wouldn't know.'

'I would say perhaps a dozen—no more than we have here. But there is this difference. They are at Zinaad.'

'And that makes a difference?'

Rucos nodded, found a stub of pencil in one pocket and used it to draw the beginnings of a map on one of the verandah's white-painted posts.

'From here Zinaad lies only some eighty kilometres—

say fifty of your miles—to the east. But it is in the High Atlas, the real mountains. Not these puny hills we have here, but where the snow-caps are year-round.' He scowled and made a small, neat cross on the post. 'Someone advised Sunner well. Zinaad is an old, abandoned Berber fortress village. It clings to the side of the rocks. There is no real road in, no people for miles. In the days of the French . . .' he stopped and shook his head. 'What matters is this. A handful could hold Zinaad against an army. Men are on their way here from Marrakech and I can have others placed to block the ways in and out of Zinaad from a distance. But—well, that is not what is wanted.'

'No.' Cord let the cigar smoulder unheeded. 'If Sunner spotted anything wrong he'd do just what he says—send us out Walt Jackson and Maggie with their throats newly cut. Maybe Mathilde too, if he hasn't already finished her. And he'd still have Sharif as his ace.'

'And Sharif still matters most to you.' It wasn't a question. Rucos grunted to himself, clearly caring little for the thought. 'Then what would you do instead?'

Cord glanced back at the house for a moment. When he faced Rucos again a strange, wisping smile creased across his face to his shadowed, stubble-edged scar.

'Someone told me once that a few men can succeed where more would fail,' he said calmly.

Rucos stared at him. 'And this someone—did he succeed?'

'No. But we might have better luck.'

Rucos chuckled. 'On this, at least, our minds work the same way. Ahmad agrees too, with some reservations. He thinks having a foreigner along is no particular help.' He switched to a soberly serious tone. 'Transport is the first

156

problem. We have the jeep—let us see what else. If I can, I will leave two men here and take the rest.'

They checked. Whatever vehicles Sunner's mercenaries had used, they'd made sure most of what was left was useless. The big Mercedes had its distributor wrecked. The same treatment had been handed out to the U.N. wagon, a small panel truck and the patrol jeep at the valley post.

'Which leaves only this.' Rucos swallowed slightly and pointed to the long, gleaming silhouette of the Rolls. 'You think...'

'We can find out.' Cord climbed aboard. There was no key in the switch but it was only a minute or so's work with a borrowed knife to by-pass wire the ignition. He pressed the starter button and the limousine whispered to dignified life. 'She'll do.'

'*Ya salaam*,' agreed Rucos almost reverently. 'We will travel like kings to a conquest—and Ahmad can bring the jeep.'

8

There is a first time for everything—and Talos Cord had never before driven a Rolls-Royce state limousine, knew it was unlikely it would happen again, and certainly not over a crazy, potholed mountain road which half the time looked like dying away into a goat-path.

But the real surprise was the dream-like ease with which the limousine's several tons of armoured weight responded to his touch. She swayed and rocked, suspension rated more for cosseting passengers in V.I.P. comfort than tackling rally-style routes, yet always transmitting the feel of a vehicle sublimely capable of coping with anything which came its way.

Gradually, as the miles crept by, Cord found himself more able to relax, to treat his charge as just another piece of transport, to find his real problem was making sure the jeep coming along behind wouldn't lose sight of their tail lights.

The feeling spread. Beside him, Major Rucos occasionally stroked the polished wood or glove-soft leather upholstery as if making sure it was real. Separated from them by the inevitable glass partition panel, the group of bulky Moroccan privates crammed into the passenger compartment gradually overcame their awe and began experimenting with switches and buttons.

For a few hectic minutes life became a circus-act comedy. Windows purred up and down. Interior lights winked and a radio blared music. A cocktail cabinet glided in and out of its coachwork recess. Finally, the internal 'phone gave an agonised squeak and Rucos had had enough. He grabbed the driving compartment receiver, blasted a torrent of fiery abuse at the luckless soldier on the other end, and gave a sniff of satisfaction as their passengers froze again among the silvered flower vases and thick pile carpets.

'Discipline,' he said with a grunt of satisfaction. 'Leave them, and they behave like children.'

The limousine rocked, his hand brushed another switch, and he gulped in alarm as the seat canted back.

'Like children,' agreed Cord, chuckling. The car took a sharp bend in a way he wouldn't have thought possible. A momentary uproar from the rear showed the army had felt the same way.

'*Ya salaam* . . .' Rucos operated the switch again and restored himself somewhat shakily to the perpendicular. 'At least we are nearly halfway.' He gathered his dignity and became serious. 'We should stop well out of sight of Zinaad. What road there is up in that valley can be seen for a long way.'

Cord nodded, checking the rear mirror for the jeep. It was about a hundred yards back. Taking one hand from the wheel, he located a cheroot from his top pocket, used one of the limousine's twin front-seat lighters, and drew on the smoke.

'The next problem is what we do when we get there. Got any ideas?'

'Perhaps.' Rucos pursed his lips. 'When men like Sunner guard a position like Zinaad they look for trouble to come from the lower slopes. They seldom think of above.' He glanced at Cord thoughtfully. 'Do you enjoy climbing?'

'Not unless I have to—and not in the middle of the damned night!'

'Then it will be interesting for us all,' murmured the Moroccan with a dry touch of humour.

.   .   .   .   .

Limousine and jeep travelled on, always deeper into the mountains, gradually climbing, headlamps glinting on patches of snow or the occasional silver of a narrow mountain torrent. Twice they glimpsed small clusters of rough stone huts, but no other trace of life, human or animal, crossed their path.

A long time seemed to pass before Rucos finally signalled him to slow. On sidelights only, the jeep now close behind, they crawled another half-mile then halted.

159

Cord followed the others out onto the track, stretching himself, shivering a little in the cold, thin mountain air, listening to the occasional clink of metal as the army men sorted themselves out, hearing the occasional crackle from the cooling exhausts. For the rest, it was a good night for what lay ahead. There was moderate moonlight, occasionally fading as a cloud wisped overhead. The wind was little more than a background whisper.

He stayed where he was, watching while Rucos talked quietly to the one N.C.O. in the group. At last, the Moroccan seemed satisfied and came over.

'To see Zinaad we have to go up there.' Rucos pointed into the darkness, towards the bleak rise of mountainside above. 'Up, then round. It is on the other side—and it is not easy.'

'I'd a feeling you were going to say that,' mused Cord wryly. 'All right, when do we start?'

'Now.' Rucos glanced at his watch, the hands glowing faintly. It was close on two a.m. 'I have told the sergeant we will need perhaps three hours to get there and back. If we have not returned by daylight it will be a problem for others. But we will take Ahmad. He knows the way best.'

Beckoned forward, the thin, grinning Berber private handed his rifle to a companion.

'He is right,' said Rucos softly. 'Where we go, a man needs both hands free and no encumbrance.'

They left the other men grouped round the vehicles and set off, leaving the track, heading towards the mountainside in single file with Cord in the middle. In a matter of minutes he'd lost all sense of bearings as they stumbled over broken rock and sudden, ankle-deep patches of snow. Sharp outcrops of quartz bit at the thin soles of his moccasins, every step demanded concentration.

Soon he was panting, the climb growing steeper, sweat running down his forehead, the pain back in his side, what little he could see around as wild and shapelessly desolate as the surface of the moon. Nothing mattered except keeping going, only his companions' heavy but regular breathing and the occasional clatter of a disturbed pebble broke the silence.

At last, Rucos signalled a halt. Cord sank down on a boulder, heard Ahmad give a soft laugh and murmur something, and managed a twisted grin in reply.

'*Kwayyis* . . . he says he is enjoying himself,' said Rucos, hunkering down beside him. 'To a mountain Berber this is the blood of life.'

'He's welcome,' said Cord wearily. 'What's next?'

'Now we start climbing,' Rucos told him calmly. 'And quietly—we will soon be very near.'

Somehow Cord managed to refrain from asking what the hell they'd just been doing. He pulled himself to his feet and nodded.

'Let's get it over with,' he said resignedly.

The next stage was a nightmare. In daylight it might have rated as little more than a tough scramble. In the night darkness only the easy certainty of his two companions kept Cord moving at a more or less respectable pace.

Patiently, Rucos and Ahmad took turns guiding his hands and feet towards finger and toe-holds on the rougher stages. Once, it was only Ahmad's thin, wiry arm which stopped him from plunging backwards from a ledge. But, suddenly, they were no longer going up but moving round the shoulder of the mountain, round and slightly down. Then they stopped, on the brink of a raw, buttress-like outcrop of rock.

Cord threw himself down, exhausted.

'Zinaad,' said Rucos, his own breath coming heavily. 'Look down there. Your friend Roder was right.'

With an effort Cord mustered the energy to crawl forward and look down. Some two hundred feet below he could make out a straggling collection of buildings, most of them small, almost flattened ruins. They were grouped round a squat, flat-roofed structure, many times bigger than the rest and separated from them by a short length of cleared, relatively level ground. Two large trucks were drawn up on the level. Just beyond, the downward slope plunged away again—leaving the whole collection in apparent imminent danger of tumbling headlong into the chasm below.

Beside him, Rucos gave a hiss of satisfaction. 'Yes, he was right. And some are awake. Captain Sunner knows his trade.'

Cord nodded. Edges of light showed from two of the old buildings. Someone hadn't been quite careful enough when it came to covering the window slits.

'Where's the road?'

Rucos pointed to the right. 'Over there. A narrow one, with a sheer drop. That is the way the French came in, but they needed artillery—and by then our men had left this way, over the mountain.'

One approach, easily held. Cord sucked gently on his teeth, putting himself in Sunner's position. A guard on the road, maybe a couple more as sentries and to guard their prisoners. But almost certainly the rest of the mercenaries would be resting—confident that their hiding-place was unknown, certain of its security.

'How long till dawn?'

'Three hours,' said Rucos. He eyed Cord carefully.

'This valley has another name among Berbers. Sometimes we call it the Place of Mists, and for a reason. As dawn comes, the air warms quickly. For a little time, as the sun starts to rise, there is always a sudden mist. Then it vanishes. When this mist happens might be a good time for us.'

'There's not likely to be better.' Cord eased himself up again, stifling a groan at the effort. 'But first we need to know what's down there. Can we make it from here?'

Rucos nodded, signalled to Ahmad, and they started off down the steep slope.

What seemed a nerve-racking age passed before they reached the first of the mud-brick ruins. But they made it unchallenged, rested for a moment in the shelter of a fallen wall, then went forward with a new, hair-trigger caution.

Ahmad's sudden warning hiss sent them scurrying into the black shadow of another tumbledown hut. A solitary figure slouched his way in their direction, the faint red glow of a cigarette between his lips.

Cord heard a soft rustle of movement, saw the long crescent-shaped knife which had appeared in Ahmad's hand, and quickly gestured it down. They hugged the shadow as the mercenary drew nearer. He passed by near enough for them to hear he was humming to himself, the machine-pistol in his grasp pointed carelessly at the ground.

'Night patrol—and bored,' murmured Rucos with a faint sigh of relief. 'Still, he can help us.'

He tapped Ahmad's shoulder. The man nodded and slipped away. Ten cold, tense minutes passed then, just as silently, he joined them again and whispered briefly.

Rucos grunted his satisfaction. 'Sunner is doing what

I would expect. He has two men at the first bend in the track. Ahmad says they have a little box with wires—at a guess I would say that means he has mined the track. Anything that comes up . . .' his hands finished the sentence, spreading in a grim, descriptive flower.

'Problem number one,' said Cord softly. 'Let's find out how many more there are.'

They inched forward again, working through the ruined huts towards the parked trucks and the flat-roofed building. The trucks were nearest, unguarded and empty. Wriggling under one, they looked out across the open ground beyond.

'Each village still has one of these places,' murmured Rucos. 'It is part citadel, part refuge and built of stone. That is why most of it still stands.'

Cord nodded, more interested in the way the pale moonlight picked out a sentry lounging on a box outside the doorway, a rifle across his knees.

'My turn.' He signalled them to wait, edged back out from under the truck, and began circling. Getting round to an angle out of view of the man at the doorway was simple enough, but he kept the Neuhausen in his hand, his ears strained for any sound of the return of the other mercenary.

At the rear of the little fortress one of the lower window-slits showed an edge of light. Cord made a final, fast, tip-toed dash across, reached the wall, and flattened himself against the rough, age-worn stonework. Something small and many-legged scurried across the rough-hewn blocks beside him and disappeared into a crack. He grimaced, went closer to the narrow window, and peered in round the edge of the piece of rough sacking which had been draped to keep the light in and the wind out.

The glow came from a kerosene lamp on the floor. Turned down low, it still showed several blanket-wrapped figures sleeping around it. Two of Sunner's men were otherwise occupied, crouched on their knees immediately beside the lamp and playing cards with an ammunition box as their table.

Cord eased back, worked his way along to the next window-slit, and tried to peer into the darkness beyond. He could hear heavy regular breathing, breathing which changed to a grunt then a sudden snore. The snore brought a low, muttered curse from somewhere close within the room.

He grinned, recognising the rumbling protest.

'Walt'—he kept his voice at little more than a whisper —'over here. Quietly.'

He heard a splutter of surprise then, while the snoring continued, a rustle of movement and a grunt of effort. Next moment Walt Jackson's face pressed against the other side of the slit, his expression incredulous.

'Cord?' The disbelief died. 'Hell, I don't know how you got here, but thank the Lord you did.'

'Who's in with you?' asked Cord in the same whisper.

'Maggie and Sharif—he's doin' the snoring.'

'Wake her, but don't disturb him.'

'Sharif?' The grunt seemed loud. 'That would take a ruddy bomb. Hold on.'

Jackson's face disappeared. Waiting, Cord stayed close to the cold stonework. He heard Jackson's voice murmur, a stifled gasp, then suddenly Maggie was staring out.

'Quietly, Maggie,' he warned softly.

She nodded her understanding. 'How did you find us?'

'It'll keep. You're all right?'

'So far.' There was screwed-down tension in her voice.

165

'We are, anyway. But I don't know what they did to Mathilde...'

Jackson eased her away from the window-slit, his face twisted in bitter anger. 'She's right. They brought Mathilde along but kept her separate. We—we heard them working her over upstairs—and that wasn't good. But what the hell's going on I don't know—we can't even get much sense out of Sharif.'

Dry-lipped, Cord nodded impatiently. 'Where is she?'

'Still up there somewhere.' It was Maggie who answered. Behind her, the snoring broke its rhythm. Sharif groaned to himself, stirred, then gradually the snoring began again. 'Talos, it was something to do with Roder. I know that much.'

'Roder's dead, Maggie.' He leaned closer. 'I've got to move. But how many men has Sunner—and where is he?'

She pointed to the floor above. 'Up there, with Sergeant Denke. I've counted eleven others with them.'

'Thirteen.' He forced a grin. 'Unlucky for somebody.'

'Let's hope it's them,' growled Jackson. 'And make sure of that skull-faced sadist, Denke. He's the one who handled Mathilde—and laughed while he did it.' He pressed forward hopefully. 'Can you get us out, Cord?'

'Not yet.'

'Got a spare gun then?'

'Soon,' he promised. The snoring ended again, and Sharif made fresh, this time positive, stirring noises. 'I'll be back. Keep quiet for now.'

A last glimpse of Maggie's face and he slipped away, circling back towards the trucks with the same infinite caution as when he'd approached. Halfway, he froze behind a pile of rubble as the one-man mercenary patrol walked past. He waited, heard the man hail the fortress sentry, gave them a moment longer, then continued on to the truck.

Rucos and Ahmad were still crouched beneath the wheels and he crawled in beside them with a sigh of relief.

'*Adiiku* . . . you were luckier than you know,' said Rucos quietly. 'There is another look-out, on the roof. We saw him just after you left.'

'You're sure?' Cord felt the hair rise on the back of his neck at the thought.

Rucos nodded, rubbing his hands together against the cold. 'We have seen him twice since then, and there is what looks like a machine-gun. It is a complication. Up there he can keep an extra watch on the road.'

One more little extra to digest. Sighing to himself, Cord told them what he'd learned, Rucos translating in a murmur for Ahmad's benefit. When he'd finished, Rucos scowled out at the night, openly dismayed.

'We have little chance.' The Moroccan chewed unhappily on his thin moustache. 'No one could bring properly armed men the way we came—not unless they were mountaineers. And the road is impossible—even without the mines, that gun on the roof is enough.' He shook his head sadly. 'My people built Zinaad with all such things in mind.'

For a moment, Cord felt infected by the same despair. Then he made a noise like a chuckle, saw the two Moroccans staring at him, and grinned reassuringly.

'Suppose we fixed the mines, and you had something like a tank?'

'Armour?' Rucos treated it like a bad joke.

'You've got the next best thing, the Rolls-Royce—you said you wanted to travel like a king to a conquest and here's the chance.' He propounded the rest of the sacrilege

167

with a gathering delight. 'The thing is armour-plated. It runs quieter than a whisper. If you waited till dawn, till that mist you talked about, you wouldn't need lights and it would take a damned good lookout to spot you.'

Suddenly, Rucos's mouth formed a silent understanding. 'On my father's life . . . yes! If you go back . . .'

'Not me. I don't know the way. And they're your men down there.'

The Moroccan scowled in protest then gave a slow nod. 'You and Ahmad—you can take care of this part?'

'There's only one way to find out.'

'True,' muttered Rucos, sighing a little. 'At dawn, then, with the mist.' He brought his watch round to his eyes and nodded. 'Two hours. There should be a signal that you are ready.'

'You'll hear one,' promised Cord. 'Then come up fast —you'll be needed.'

Rucos whispered for a moment in Ahmad's ear then rolled round again. 'He knows what we have decided'— he drew a deep breath—'and for the rest, may Allah favour us.'

Cord watched him edge back from under the truck. Almost immediately, he disappeared. A pebble rustled somewhere, then all was still again.

.   .   .   .   .

Dawn comes quickly in North Africa. But there is a warning, a time of grey quarter-light when moon and stars seem to struggle against the need to surrender.

Long before then Cord felt restless. Muscles chilled and cramped by the tedious yet nerve-racking wait, the pain in his side gathering again, he'd come to know the guard routine around Zinaad as if he was part of it.

The man on night patrol would share a cigarette with the sentry at the fortress door then head off towards the post overlooking the track. He'd be gone fifteen minutes then would wander back again for another low-voiced gossip, usually of the same duration. The mercenary on the roof was either anti-social or made of more disciplined material. He moved rarely, called down only a couple of times to his companions, and spent most of his time apparently wrapped in a blanket beside the dark hump of the gun.

At last Cord felt a tap on his shoulder and Ahmad pantomimed they should move. He backed out willingly, following the Berber on a stomach-and-elbows crawl to one of the tumbledown huts on the outskirts of the derelict village. The little Berber squatted down, winked cheerfully, and pointed in the direction of the track.

'Not yet.' Quickly, Cord shook his head. The patrol was due unless for once he'd changed his monotonous schedule.

They waited what seemed a long time, almost too long a time, before the man passed by. More minutes ticked away and the first hint of grey was edging into the sky before he returned. Cord let him get safely on his way towards the old fortress then nodded.

A grin on his face, Ahmad led the way for about two hundred yards then stopped and pointed.

The post was just ahead, a few large boulders and some other debris dragged together at the side of the track. Facing down it, the two mercenaries who manned it were little more than vague silhouettes. One sat on the ground with his back to them, the other leaned against the low breastwork in half-asleep watch.

Cord felt a brief sense of pity for them then it washed

away with a sudden tide of memories. Palombo shot down beside him. Peterley who must have been glad to die. Roder—and perhaps Mathilde. They were only the ones he knew about.

'*Aywa?*' Ahmad nudged him, knife in hand. 'Now?'

'Now,' he agreed softly.

They went in fast and quiet, were almost on top of the men before some sixth sense made them start to turn. Cord took the figure on the ground as he tried to rise. Right arm round the man's throat, left hand clamped over his mouth, Cord forced the struggling mercenary down again.

The man threshed and rolled, trying to bite through the hand sealing his lips. Slowly, steadily, Cord increased the pressure on his neck and felt the threshing become more convulsive then weaken and cease. Grimly, he kept the strangle-lock for a full minute longer then let go.

Eyes staring, face still contorted, the man was dead. Vaguely sick, Cord lowered him to the ground and looked round. Ahmad was a few feet away, calmly cleaning his knife. The second mercenary lay crumpled against the boulders.

In the sky to the east the grey was firming fast, an edge of light appearing behind it. Down below, Rucos by now would have his men packed in the Rolls-Royce, waiting for the promised signal. He had to work fast.

The detonator box was set at safe, but he carefully unclipped the wires from their terminals before he traced the rest of the thin cable, coiling it over one as he went. Sixty yards down he reached the end. The mine, the size of a shoe-box but twice as heavy, lay in a shallow hole scraped into the gravel surface. Sunner's men hadn't bothered to cover it.

He lifted it in both hands and hurried back to collect Ahmad. The Berber eyed the mine nervously but picked up the detonator box and the mercenaries' machine-pistols then followed.

Rucos wanted a signal. And he was going to get one. Sweating now, Cord tried to keep a grip on caution as he set a fast, half-crouching pace back to the parked trucks. Wriggling under the nearest, he laid the shoe-box mine beneath the smooth belly of its fuel tank. He checked that the sentry ahead hadn't moved, then went back the way he'd come, paying out the cable.

It finished just at the empty doorway of a roofless hut. Feverishly, fingers suddenly clumsy, he took the detonator box from Ahmad and clipped the wires back on their terminals. The switch clicked smoothly to 'Ready' but he moved it back again. There was one thing more to be done.

Waving Ahmad to stay, Cord collected one of the machine-pistols and crawled off again, heading for the blind side of the fortress. Once, when he stopped, he had a clear view of the man on the roof. The mercenary was moving around up there, silhouetted against the brightening sky.

But man and building seemed oddly blurred. Suddenly, he realised why. Rucos's mist was coming, heralding the warmth of day, forming as air and earth released their overnight moisture.

He hurried on and reached the window-slit. They'd been waiting—Jackson's face peered out immediately, his hands took the machine-pistol with loving delight.

'Use it only if they try to reach you,' Cord told him in a fast whisper. 'Better wake Sharif now.'

'He's awake already,' grunted Jackson. 'I told him I'd tear his guts out if he as much as sneezed . . .'

'Maggie . . .'

'Here.' She appeared at the slit and Jackson edged back.

'It'll start once you hear a bang. Keep low and keep hoping the rest works.'

She looked at him for a moment, saying nothing, then nodded gravely.

.　　　.　　　.　　　.　　　.

By the time he got back to the hut and sank down beside the detonator box, the mist was a thickening reality.

'Ahmad . . .' his voice died away. The Berber had gone, the second machine-pistol lay propped against the hut wall.

Cord peered out of the sagging doorway, listening, hearing nothing, yet understanding—and cursing himself for having forgotten the one vital factor that remained.

The patrolman. He would be on his rounds again, heading towards the track and the post with the two dead men. Ahmad had seen him pass, had realised, had gone off after him . . .

Briefly, he was tempted to turn that detonator handle, press down the T-bar switch, give the signal. He fought it down, reached for the machine-pistol instead, and checked it grimly. It was a nine mil. Sterling, the curved magazine on its left side fully loaded, the cold metal of the skeleton butt a comfort on its own.

Something rustled near at hand. He heard the sound again, brought the Sterling round to cover the doorway, then relaxed with a sigh as Ahmad's thin, slight figure crawled the last few feet and flopped down beside him.

The Berber had a long, clawed gash down one side of his face. His khaki tunic was torn. But he was still grinning as if he knew no other expression—and he was carrying another Sterling.

'*Kwayyis* . . . is fine.' The man struggled to shape the unfamiliar words. 'That Sunner's man'—he drew a hopeful, expressive finger across his throat—'okay?'

'Okay,' said Cord thankfully. He was still gripping the Sterling as though it was part of him. Gently, he laid the weapon down.

What mattered now was timing. The light and the mist against the minutes before the patrolman should have come wandering back from the track-edge post to check at the fortress. Calculate one against the other, calculate to the limit. He could already see things clearly inside the hut—and outside the building the mist was now a wet, rolling fog. He used the sixty-yard distance to the truck as his measure—and even as he watched another, thicker bank of grey tendrilled over it.

Four minutes more, and the mist cloaked the truck like a strange opalescent veil in the gathering dawn. The sun would be edging up. When it did, that mist would melt . . .

Carefully, his brain suddenly ice-cold, all tension gone now he was committed, Cord moved the detonator switch from 'Safe', let it click against the 'Ready' stop, and reached for the T-bar. Ahmad looked, swallowed, and flattened himself on the hut floor.

The T-bar went down with a faint sigh of tension springs. Unseen contacts met, bridged, completed their circuit.

First the instant blossom of orange-white fury, then the blast. Deafened, feeling the air sucked from his lungs, Cord saw the truck jerk bodily in the air then fall almost slowly. The hut shook, debris pattered—and as the truck crashed on its side there was a second explosion, duller yet more penetrating as the fuel tank went up. Flames seared skyward. More debris pattered down inside the hut, debris and a scattered, scurrying assortment of insect life from spiders on.

'Out. Make it fast.' He grabbed Ahmad's shoulder, jerked the wiry Berber bodily to his feet, and grabbed the machine-pistol with his other hand.

Smoke was joining the flames as they ran at a fast crouch, making for the downward slope, hearing the first cries of alarm give way to shouted orders. Cord led the way, heading in a wide curve, slithering down the start of the slope then along its edge, pulling Ahmad flat against the broken, jagged rock as figures appeared briefly in the mist.

'Move that other truck—fast, damn you!' Sunner's high-pitched voice made itself heard above the rest. 'Get going unless you ruddy fools want to walk out of this place.' He shouted again, a new urgency in his voice. 'Hagan—take Kronbar and check those huts. Shoot on sight.'

His voice was still echoing as Cord scrambled off again, Ahmad at his heels. Through the swirling fog, eerily laced with reflected colour between the blazing truck and the orange glow of the rising sun, they heard the bark of the second truck's engine. Then the fortress loomed ahead, its door was unguarded, they were racing towards it.

To the man on the roof they appeared like wraiths out of nowhere. By the time he'd reacted and had the machine-gun swung round and down to maximum depression they were less than twenty yards from their goal.

One long, wild burst stitched along the ground behind them—then the gun could no longer bear, they had tumbled through the door, into an empty hallway and

Ahmad was down on the floor with the Sterling pointing out into the mist.

There were two doors, an archway and a narrow, winding stairway leading to the upper floor. The other side of the archway was a broad hall strewn with blankets and other equipment left by Sunner's men. One of the doors lay open, the entrance to a dark, evil-smelling cellar. The other was fastened by a stout wooden bar and double socket. He jerked the bar loose, remembered his own warning, and shouted his name.

'We heard . . .' the door swung open and Jackson peered out, face tight with suspicion, the machine-pistol ready. He saw Cord, beamed, then suddenly stared and swung the Sterling's muzzle, triggering as it came.

The long burst came close to shaving Cord's side. As it died there was a clatter from the stairway. A blue-clad figure came tumbling down the last steps as Cord turned, then sprawled motionless on the stone floor, a pistol at its side.

'Thanks,' said Cord feebly.

'My pleasure, Mr Cord,' grinned Jackson. 'All right, you two—come on out.'

Maggie emerged quickly, her face pale but her eyes bright. Behind her and apparently determined to stay that way, a bedraggled, scared-looking Mohammed Sharif peered anxiously around.

'We've another gun,' said Jackson, gesturing towards the pistol. 'Sharif—no, you better have it, Maggie. Know how to use one?'

She nodded, moistening her lips. 'Talos, what about Mathilde?'

Before he could speak Ahmad grunted a warning from the doorway, sighted along his barrel, and sent a short

175

burst rasping out into the mist. There was a high-pitched yelp of pain, a snarled command, and the air was torn by a ragged torrent of answering fire.

Lead spat and whined off the stone walls as they threw themselves flat. Sharif gave a squeal of fright as a spent bullet nicked his shoulder and made an immediate, crab-like scuttle back where he'd come from.

'Walt'—as the firing died, Cord thumbed towards the doorway—'give him a hand. That's Sunner's only way back in. I'll check up top.'

He started for the stairs. On his way up, the firing began again from outside.

Rucos should be on the way. Rucos had to be on the way. He reached the upper floor, a vast central, shadow-filled hall with a warren of tiny cubicles leading off. Starting from the right he moved along them quickly, kicking open the few doors still hanging, the Sterling ready.

The third held a camp bed, a metal despatch box lying beside it . . . but that could wait.

The next was empty. The next again—he shoved the door open, swore softly, and lowered the Sterling.

Mathilde Dolanne lay on her back, gagged, tied spread-eagle to an old, warped wooden bedframe. Only a few rags still clung to that beautiful, bronze body. What had been done to her he couldn't guess. There were no obvious marks. But a pair of dark eyes stared at him in a mixture of fear and terror. As he moved closer she seemed to try to shrink back, moaning behind the gag.

'Take it easy, Mathilde,' he soothed.

Firing racketed again from outside and was answered by a flurry of single shots from below. The girl twitched in fresh panic.

'Mathilde, it's all right.' Quickly, he loosened the gag's

knot with one hand and pulled it free.

She screamed, a frantic, unintelligible sound.

As it faded, someone laughed.

Cord spun round in a crouch, staring out at the big, empty central room. Behind him, Mathilde screamed again and this time the word came through.

'Roof . . .'

He looked up at the high, cobwebbed ceiling, saw the half-opened hatch above, the skull-tight, contorted face leering down at him. Sergeant Denke had an automatic in his hand, his thin, bloodless lips drawn back in anticipation. Cord knew he couldn't swing the Sterling up fast enough but sheer reflex hope made him try.

Denke's knuckle tightened and a shot snarled—but not from his gun. It spat orange flame a second later, fired as he instinctively flinched from the bullet which smashed splinters from the wooden hatchway inches from his head.

The mercenary's bullet flew wide, yet still found a target. Cord heard the stifled, sighing moan behind him at the same instant as the Sterling's muzzle came into line.

The machine-pistol began bucking in his hands, hosing up at that suddenly jerking, flopping obscenity above. Hate and fury kept his finger jammed to the trigger, unable to stop even when Denke pitched forward, his body hanging limp yet refusing to fall, one foot jammed between hatch and hatchway.

The magazine clicked empty. The echo of the shots faded, leaving only the acrid smell of cordite and a litter of spilled, rolling cartridge cases.

His hands were shaking. He let the Sterling fall with a clatter and looked round. Maggie Delday stood at the top of the stairway, staring at the dangling figure, horror in her eyes, the pistol she'd used held her limply by her side.

'I heard her scream . . .' her voice trailed away, the rest unnecessary.

Cord swallowed hard and turned towards the cubicle. One glance was enough. Denke's bullet had hit Mathilde high in the soft tissue of the neck, angling in. There was only a tiny round hole.

She must have died instantly. He hoped so—her face, at least, had relaxed into a hard-won peace. Cord felt Maggie at his side, looked at her wordlessly, then another fierce burst of firing from outside jerked him back to reality. It was followed by the sudden, harsh blast of a grenade. Ahmad and Jackson were still answering with single shots, conserving what ammunition they'd left.

Where the hell was Rucos? If Sunner had more of those grenades . . .

But there was that machine-gun on the roof. How had it got up there?

The second hatch was in the far corner, reached by a rickety ladder. He reached it at a run, clawed up the rungs, shoved the hatch back bodily with his shoulders, and scrambled through.

Alone on the roof, the mist now ebbing fast, Cord crawled forward and looked down on the rest of the village. A blue-clad figure lay still near the burning truck. He could see others firing from cover, men who showed themselves briefly, professionals who moved fast and purposefully.

The gun, an American M.60, glinting like new, waited on its aluminium tripod mounting with the barrel still depressed. The cold butt-plate cuddled tight against his shoulder, he reached for the pistol grip, brought the sights in line, then stopped.

Dust-covered, bouncing like some wild cross-country

jeep, the great black bulk of the Roll-Royce sped out of the wisping fog towards them. It travelled silent as a ghost then, as the limousine reached the first of the huts, there was a sudden, trumpeting, non-stop bray from its aristocratic twin horns.

A mercenary appeared in front of it, firing from the hip. One headlamp glass smashed. The car smoothly altered course, didn't slow, and that massive, old-fashioned silver radiator hit the man like a battering ram, tossing him aside.

It came on fast, jolting over rubble with disdain, horn still sounding, suddenly the only target that existed for Sunner's men. A grenade bounced off the windshield, exploded, and still it came on, emerging from the dust swaying but intact.

Broadside to the old fortress it braked to a stop. Doors flew open and Rucos's Moroccans came tumbling out—silent, khaki-clad figures in a vengeful mood.

For Sunner's remaining men the sight was enough. First one then suddenly all of them fell back. What began as a scattering changed to a desperate bid to escape. Cord held his fire, weary of killing. And he didn't seem needed. He saw one terrified quarry knocked down by a bullet, start to rise again—then the flash of a bayonet as a Moroccan finished the job.

It was brutal, it was thorough—and from the fortress roof somehow a thing detached from reality, those figures running below like so many jerking puppets.

Except for Sunner. Cord saw him a moment later, bareheaded, that short, thickset figure and fleshy face unmistakable. Crouching behind a low section of broken mud-brick wall, hidden from ground-level view, the man started to rise, his right hand coming back clutching the black egg-shape of a grenade. Less than twenty yards away, still standing beside the Rolls-Royce, Rucos was oblivious of the threat as he watched the hunt.

In one smooth, almost unhurried process Cord sighted and triggered. The M.60 snarled a two-second burst of rasping cyclic staccato. Sunner staggered, swayed, spun round in slow-motion and fell. As he went down, the grenade spilled from his hand in a feeble, aimless arc and rolled a few yards.

It exploded as Rucos dived for cover. The Moroccan got up slowly, brushed some dust from his tunic, glanced from Sunner's body up to where Cord still waited, and gave a calm nod of thanks.

.   .   .   .   .

The last shots were fired five minutes later, high up on the mountainside.

Cord quit the roof. Down below, Mathilde's body was being moved and he was glad. But there was still that little camera in his pocket, still a promise to be fulfilled. Wearily, he moved on to the cubicle where he'd seen the despatch box then stopped, mouth tightening.

Mohammed Sharif was already there, down on his knees beside the opened box, pawing feverishly through its contents.

'Important stuff?' asked Cord softly.

The Arab glanced round quickly, saw him, and gave a nervous nod. When he spoke, there was a sharp quivering urgency in his voice.

'State papers, Cord. The—the box has been opened. There is one most important document missing.'

'You're sure?' Cord leaned against the doorway, his manner unhurried.

Sharif's old arrogance flared back to the surface. 'Of course I'm sure, you . . .' he stopped short and swallowed hard, switching to a milder tone. 'Mr Cord, you have done well. Jemma is grateful. But this document must be found.' Again he pawed through the box then sank back on his heels, with a sound like a groan.

'Not there?' queried Cord sympathetically.

'No.' Sharif chewed hard on his lip. 'Unless—unless Sunner had it with him!' He started to his feet. 'I must look . . .'

'Out there?' Cord eased out and blocked the doorway. 'A man might still stop a stray bullet in the open. Let's not risk that happening, Your Excellency—not this late. Suppose you wait and let me try.'

'You?' Sharif considered the matter, torn between possibilities. At last, he nodded. 'Search his body, yes. But whatever you find must be brought straight to me, unopened. It—ah—it is a matter of State security.'

'And you can trust me,' said Cord solemnly.

He kept a deliberate, ambling pace down the worn stone stairway and went outside. Sunner's body lay where it had fallen, fleshy lips drawn back in a final grimace. Cord sighed, bent down, and reached for the man's tunic.

'Would you rob the dead?' asked an amused voice in mock horror.

He glanced round, saw Rucos, and grinned.

'President Sharif happens to have lost something. I—well, I said I'd help look for it.'

'A kindly thought,' said Rucos dryly. He crooked a finger. 'Perhaps you would look at this car first—the other side. There is some damage to the paintwork which concerns me.'

Cord stared at him then understood. 'If that's how you feel, I'd better.'

They went round together, the car shielding them from the fortress. Casually, Rucos reached into his inside pocket and brought out an oblong envelope. There was a bullet-hole through one corner, the edges were stained with blood.

'He had this. I was—well, uncertain what to do with it.'

The agreement comprised one sheet of heavy parchment. In return for 'major assistance' the sum of four million dollars would be paid to Mohammed Sharif over a six-year period, beginning on the day 'agreement covering exclusive rutile mineral rights in present and future territory of the Republic of Jemma' was completed and finalised.

The signatures at the bottom were all the rest that was needed.

The little camera made a cheerful clicking sound. Cord took some extra frames to be sure, then Rucos returned the sheet to its envelope.

'President Sharif will be impatient,' said Rucos solemnly, handing it over. 'For the rest—I feel the excitement has affected my memory.'

Cord slipped the envelope inside his shirt. Bright sunshine was pouring down on the valley, the Moroccans were drifting back. 'Any casualties?'

'Only two I know about—neither serious.'

'Sunner's men?'

Rucos's mouth twisted a little with an awkward embarrassment. He said nothing, but shook his head.

Cord didn't press him. The Moroccans had had a score of their own to settle.

.   .   .   .   .

They made a further brief pretence of inspecting the car then left it. Cord returned to Sunner's body and went through the motions of emptying the pockets. It was easy enough to slip the envelope into the collection, then he returned to the fortress. Pouncing on him at the doorway, Sharif snatched the envelope, examined it in a corner, and immediately blossomed affability.

'This is what was missing!' He beamed around. 'Now all that remains is to leave this place. What arrangements have been made?'

'That's why we were looking at the car,' said Cord neutrally. 'Rucos will get it tidied up a little. Then maybe Your Excellency would prefer to spend the day resting comfortably. You could go back to Mihmaaz and still leave as scheduled for Jemma tomorrow.'

Sharif nodded enthusiastic agreement. 'I need time to recover,' he said plaintively. 'My secretary, my closest adviser—both plotting against me. Who can a man trust?' His eyes narrowed a little. 'Even one of your U.N. drivers was involved.'

'As much to our surprise as your own,' Cord assured him.

'And you have more than made amends.' Sharif brightened again and dismissed the matter with an attempt at grace.

Cord dodged further thanks, ran the gauntlet of Walt Jackson's exuberant back-slapping, and went in search of Maggie.

She was alone in a shadowed room at the back of the old building, sitting on a box and smoking a cigarette. When she saw him, she ran a hand through her short, fair hair and smiled wanly.

'All over?' she asked.

'Uh-huh.' Cord went behind her and put his hands on her shoulders. She sighed a little and let her head rest back against him.

'Mathilde was—well, different from what I thought. Wasn't she, Talos?'

'Something very different. Sharif doesn't know how different yet—but he'll find out, the hard way.'

She turned her head and looked up at him.

'And you? What happens now?'

He said nothing for a moment. Rucos was radioing for a helicopter, to evacuate his wounded. There would be space on it for him on the return flight to Marrakech.

Somehow Cord had a feeling he might take the film on from there himself. Abdul Zieull had a right to know how Roder Hassabou Zieull had died—and to hear of Mathilde and the rest.

When Mohammed Sharif returned home he was going to find life held some surprises.

'There's some tidying up to be done,' he said carefully. 'Then I can get back here for a little while. A day or so, anyway.' He grinned a little and rasped a thumb over the stubble of beard on his face. 'I'll get rid of this along the way. All right?'

Her eyes told him it would be.